OTHER
Harlequin Romances
by ELIZABETH ASHTON

Many of these titles are available at your local bookseller
or through the Harlequin Reader Service.

For a free catalogue listing all available Harlequin Romances,
send your name and address to:

HARLEQUIN READER SERVICE,
M.P.O. Box 707, Niagara Falls, N.Y. 14302
Canadian address: Stratford, Ontario, Canada N5A 6W2

or use order coupon at back of book

Cousin Mark

by

ELIZABETH ASHTON

Harlequin Books

TORONTO • LONDON • NEW YORK • AMSTERDAM • SYDNEY

Original hardcover edition published in 1971
by Mills & Boon Limited

ISBN 0-373-01534-8

Harlequin edition published October 1971

Second printing February 1976
Third printing March 1978

Printed in U.S.A.

CHAPTER ONE

'IT's the most preposterous arrangement I've ever heard of!'

Helen Carew, self-possessed and self-effacing, had long learned the wisdom of keeping her opinions to herself in an employer's house, but the terms of her late master's will had startled her out of her usual reticence, and besides, she was no longer employed.

The solicitor, Albert Preston, dry and leathery as his own briefcase, threw her a nervous glance, took his glasses off and polished them.

'No doubt my late client thought he was making a wise provision for the child,' he said mildly, 'but his ideas were far behind the times; however, you need not distress yourself, I doubt if that clause is binding upon either of the parties concerned.'

He put his spectacles back upon his nose and glanced at the person involved. Damaris Treherne was sitting forlornly in the window embrasure, where the fitful gleams of sunlight coming through the diamond panes struck points of fire amid the copper hair that curled round her small, pale face, in which were set wide-spaced eyes—strange green-grey eyes, cat's eyes flecked with gold, that had a luminous quality. In her skimpy black dress she looked no more than a child, and Mr. Preston doubted if the significance of what he had told her had penetrated the shell of grief that enclosed her.

Damaris Treherne of Ravenscrag in the County of Cornwall was the last direct descendant of Sir Hugh Treherne, who had been a prominent figure in the local scene for over half a century. Her parents had died when she was a baby and she had been reared by Mrs.

5

Garth, the motherly housekeeper, herself a widow, who had supervised the running of the Manor ever since Sir Hugh had lost his wife, whom Damaris could barely remember. She had been assisted by a string of governesses, of whom Helen Carew was the last and most efficient, also she was the only one who had won any affection from her pupil.

Predominant in Damaris' short life had been her grandfather. She had been his constant companion since her earliest years, he had taught her to ride and to swim, and had imbued in her an intense love of the county of her birth, its folk lore and traditions, with which her own family history was mingled. The baronet as he aged became a little eccentric and a complete recluse. His books, his dogs, his horses and his granddaughter's company contented him. He stayed hale and hearty until his last illness, and that need not have proved fatal if he had taken care of himself, but Sir Hugh had always scorned physical weakness and refused to be cosseted; eventually he succumbed, and suddenly, to a coronary thrombosis, leaving behind him a desolate slip of a girl.

As yet Damaris had been unable to realise her loss, The sudden death, followed by the funeral, which was attended by a crowd of strangers, who wanted to honour the passing of the baronet who had ignored them for the latter part of his life, had seemed unreal, and now Mr. Preston's efforts to explain how she was left had little reality either. Actually she knew that Sir Hugh had left the Manor to his great-nephew, who would in any case inherit the title, the old man had told her so. She knew also of the stipulation attached to the bequest that had so upset her governess. Mark Treherne belonged to a branch of the family that had settled in South America, with whom Sir Hugh had lost touch.

'Granddad said Ravenscrag would always be my home,' she said a little anxiously, for she loved the place; it was her whole world since she had never been further afield.

Mr. Preston glanced nervously at Helen Carew and cleared his throat; 'It was in the hope that it would always be so that Sir Hugh made this ... er ... peculiar stipulation.'

He had remonstrated with his client when he had drawn up the will, but Sir Hugh had insisted. Ravenscrag should belong to the next baronet, and Damaris would need a protector. The best person to take charge of her was a husband. He had left the Manor to Mark Treherne on condition that he took Damaris to wife.

'I hope Cousin Mark won't mind having to marry me,' Damaris said childishly, thereby betraying that she had understood the solicitor's explanation.

Mr. Preston looked sympathetically at the girl's white face, in which the dark-ringed eyes looked enormous. Sir Hugh had been very wrong, he thought, to keep her isolated upon the estate. He was unaware that the old man had been revolted by the specimens of modern youth who flooded the West Country in the summertime, unable to believe that beneath their strange garb and flowing locks the cardinal virtues could still exist. Lurid accounts in the newspapers of the doings of popular singers, university malcontents and drug imbibers confirmed him in his assumption that young people of today were decadent, ill-mannered and undisciplined, so he would not permit Damaris to mingle with them, even by going to school, nor was she encouraged to read the papers. When he engaged Helen Carew, he told her that his granddaughter was to be educated to be a lady and kept away from all contaminating influences. Then, belatedly realising that she was ill-equipped to face the world, he had bequeathed her to his heir, confident that Mark would take care of her.

Helen said angrily, 'He's being bribed to marry you. Ravenscrag is a fine old place and its antiquity will

7

appeal to an American.' She turned to the solicitor. 'But perhaps he's already committed? It's unlikely a man as old as he is won't have considered matrimony.'

'Sir Mark is unwed,' Mr. Preston said shortly, disliking the word bribed, while Damaris winced at the use of the title that had been her grandfather's, 'and I've no idea how old he is. He cabled that he regretted he was unable to attend the funeral. We are of course acquainting him with the terms of the will. The rest is up to him.'

'Sir Hugh has been very generous to me,' Helen remarked; she had been left a useful sum which would enable her to fulfil a long-cherished dream, a partnership with a friend who was starting a gift shop in a nearby small sea-port. but she would have gladly forgone it, to make Damaris' future more satisfactory. 'Has Damaris nothing of her own if Sir Mark refuses to honour this absurd stipulation?'

'She will have a small income from her mother's marriage settlement,' Mr. Preston told them, 'and the capital becomes hers when she's twenty-one. Meanwhile, Sir Mark and myself are her trustees.' He glanced again at the still figure on the window seat. 'How old are you now, my dear?'

'Eighteen.'

'Really? How the years fly!' She looks about fifteen, he thought, and wondered what on earth Sir Mark Treherne would make of her. He had heard rumours about that gentlemen, who, though he had never visited Ravenscrag when he came to Europe, had made a splash in Paris and Monte Carlo. The *estancia* in Argentina, it seemed, paid dividends. Some compromise would have to be effected, for the sophisticated man of the world did not sound like a suitable mate for the pale little orphan crouched on the window seat, and he rather doubted if Sir Hugh's condition would hold water in a court of law.

'Then she's independent,' Helen said with relief.

'She needn't fulfil this ridiculous bargain.'

Damaris compressed her lips into a firm line. 'Grand-dad said I was to marry Cousin Mark.'

'You're too young to think of marrying anyone,' Helen said sharply.

'I'm eighteen,' Damaris reminded her, 'and of course I must fulfil Granddad's wishes.'

The man and the woman exchanged glances and the solicitor raised his shoulders in a slight shrug. Damaris' obstinacy might make difficulties.

'Well, we'll have to wait for Sir Mark's instructions,' he said, closing his briefcase. 'It will take a little time to get probate, of course,' he glanced at Helen, 'you'll stay here, Miss Carew, until you get your money?'

'I'll stay with Damaris as long as she needs me,' Helen promised.

Damaris asked anxiously, 'Will Cousin Mark be coming soon?'

'I hope so,' Mr. Preston told her, 'we need to consult him. Now, don't worry, my dear, I'm sure everything will turn out all right.'

He wanted to be reassuring, but he foresaw many complications, unaware that Damaris was not worried at all. Her grandfather had loved and protected her, and in his infinite wisdom he had left her to Cousin Mark, knowing he would also love and protect her; it was as simple as that.

As he took the small brown hand that Damaris extended towards him, Mr. Preston was mentally condemning his late client for his selfishness in not sending Damaris to school and college, and allowing her to develop normally. Now that she was standing beside him, he realised with faint surprise that she was nearly as tall as he was; he was a man of medium height. A lifetime of dealing with human follies had hardened him, but the naïve innocence of the girl's eyes, raised candidly to his, went straight to his heart, awakening a softness that rarely troubled him when dealing with his

9

clients.

'I'll be here to look after you,' he assured her. 'Come to me in any difficulty. Remember I also am one of your trustees.' Still holding her hand, he asked her curiously; 'Did your grandfather ever mention this ... er ... matrimonial project to you?'

'Yes, several times just lately.'

Only a few evenings before his death, Sir Hugh had spoken to her about her future.

'I shan't be here much longer, Damaris,' he had said, 'but you need not worry about what will happen to you. I've provided for that.'

She had cried out that she could not bear to contemplate a future without him and he must not talk of dying. Gently he had soothed her and gone on.

'As you know the title is entailed upon the next male heir, and that is your Cousin Mark. The holder of the title must live here, and the place needs a man to run it; I fear I've neglected it of late, but you shall not be dispossessed, I know how you love the Manor. The solution is a marriage between you and Mark. I shall write and ask him to come and stay and we can discuss it.'

He had never told her much about their South American connections, but that night he became expansive. His brother, being a younger son, had gone to seek his fortune in the New World. He had married a rich woman and they had bought the *estancia* in Argentina.

'Your parents were flying out to see him when they were killed,' he told her sombrely. 'Up till then I had hoped for a grandson. I met my nephew at the funeral. He was a well set up young man, but I didn't like his wife, who was an Argentinian. I've seen none of them since, and now he's dead too, so the title will be Mark's. I don't know if there are any more of them. I believe there's a girl, but it's only Mark we're concerned with. He must be quite a bit older than you are, for his

10

father married young, and it's time we made his acquaintance.'

But there was no time; Sir Hugh had waited too long. A week later he was dead.

As Damaris admitted her knowledge, Helen made a movement of surprise. 'You never told me, Damaris,' she said reproachfully. Had she known, she might have been able to reason with the old man.

'I . . . I didn't want to talk about it . . . I couldn't bear to think of Granddad dying, but he told me Cousin Mark would come and look after me so I wouldn't be alone.' She smiled sadly. 'He said he could comfort me.'

Mr. Preston privately thought that that was the last thing the new baronet would be likely to do. What he would need would be a sophisticated wife to run his fine house and act as hostess to his friends, not an undeveloped girl who would need infinite patience and understanding before she would be fit to occupy the position required of her. Nothing of this showed in his face as he patted the hand he still held.

'Goodbye, my dear, I'll be seeing you again soon.'

'Thank you for coming and explaining everything,' she said politely.

Helen accompanied him to his car and took the opportunity to enlarge upon her feelings about the situation. A lonely woman, plain and middle-aged, she had concentrated her starved affections upon her charge, and was appalled at the predicament in which the girl had been placed. The solicitor pointed out that the clause need not necessarily be enforced if the parties concerned could arrive at a settlement which did not include marriage. He suspected that living for so long in isolation, Sir Hugh had allowed his wishes to out run his common sense. The girl seemed willing enough, but Sir Mark's reaction was unpredictable. Helen continued to feel outraged that Damaris should be handed over with the property like a parcel of goods. She was convinced that if the new owner did agree to marry her pupil it would be only to strengthen his title to the estate; moreover, Mark Treherne was half Latin-American, which, she considered made him suspect. Latins were proverbially untrustworthy with women. Something of all this she tried to explain tactfully to Damaris, but found she was up against a stone wall. The girl thought of her cousin as a slightly younger edition of her grandfather. She knew that marriage entailed rather more than fatherly affection, but since Mark was apparently nearly middle-aged, she imagined he would be past making amatory advances and all he would expect would be the companionship that she had given to the older man. She loved her home passionately, and her grandfather's wish, since it was the last he had expressed, was sacred to her. So she was completely impervious to Helen's hints and suggestions.

'Grandfather knew all about Cousin Mark,' she insisted, 'and whoever his mother was, he's a Treherne, but of course Granddad wouldn't have discussed him with you—he's family.'

A remark which annoyed Helen.

'He knew what was best for me,' Damaris went on. 'I trust his judgment entirely, even though he ... he's dead.'

Helen could say no more, but she hoped fervently that Damaris would not be too painfully disillusioned when Mark came.

However, days passed and Mark Treherne delayed his arrival; in the interim, Damaris began to recover from the shock of her grandfather's death. Every stick and stone of the estate recalled his memory, and wandering alone with her two dogs, or riding her chestnut mare Sheba to and fro from each favourite spot, it seemed to her that he was still with her. Often out of the tail of her eye, she thought that she glimpsed the tall, lean figure, unbent by age, the thick white hair, the gleaming dark eyes, and only when she turned her head did she realise that he was not physically present, but she was sure that he was with her in spirit and the thought comforted her. She belonged to an old people, a superstitious people, a people who for many centuries had been a race apart, and if she believed that her grandfather's ghost met her in the lonely places, there were not many of the country people who would not believe her.

She was a familiar figure among the tenant farmers and cottagers, who had watched her grow from a toddler to a teenager, and they always greeted her with warmth, restrained by the deference due to the daughter of the Manor. She was friendly but not intimate with them; she looked upon them as her people, to whom she owed a responsibility. That they had been bequeathed to Cousin Mark was hard to stomach, but she was resolved that she would not let him usurp her place among them.

Ravenscrag Manor was a low grey stone house with a slate roof, built in a fold of the undulating countryside, where it was sheltered from the prevailing westerly winds blowing in straight from the Atlantic. On either side slopes rose from the miniature valley with farmhouses near their summits, while below the garden a small rivulet ran along the valley floor, which was so narrow that it was more like a cleft in the hills, to end in a cascade when it reached the cliffs which, tall and forbidding, guarded access to a shaley beach, with no inviting stretch of yellow sand to attract tourists, who were deterred by alarming notices, warning of the dangers of the crumbling cliffs.

Damaris, sure-footed as a goat, had made her own secret path down to the inhospitable shore. Once below the grey wall of cliff, she would sit for hours watching the creaming tide slowly enfold the ragged rocks, that ran in perpendicular black ridges, far out into the sea, a saw-toothed menace to shipping. While she dreamed, her two dogs would hunt ecstatically and un-successfully for seagulls' nests. They were black lab-radors, called Tristan and Isolde, which had become abbreviated to Tris and Sol. She had named them for one of her favourite stories, that of the ill-fated Cornish Queen, Iseult—Wagner's version Isolde was easier to pronounce—who had loved the young knight who had brought her from Ireland as a result of drinking the love potion designed for her husband, King Mark. The end of the tragedy had several versions, and she knew them all; it was her most frequent reading.

Sitting one day in her favourite haunt on a blue and gold day, the restless breeze for once quiescent, Damaris was roused from her reverie by the sound of falling stones, followed by a frantic barking from the dogs. Jumping to her feet, she saw that someone had been trying to climb down the cliff and had ended igno-miniously in a slide of shale, while Tris and Sol, resent-ing this intrusion, were baying at the prostrate figure excitedly.

Her first feeling was resentment that her privacy had been invaded, then realising that if she did not inter-vene there might be damage done by her over-zealous defenders, she ran to the rescue.

'Tris! Sol! Sit!'

Reluctantly the dogs abandoned their quarry and obediently sat with wary eyes fixed on the trespasser. Damaris looked down upon the long length of a young man, who was dazedly trying to raise himself.

'Are you hurt?'

He struggled into a sitting position, and looked at himself ruefully. He was plentifully sprinkled with dust and earth, and the blue tee-shirt he wore was torn in several places; the tougher canvas shorts were un-damaged.

'No, I don't think so, but I thought those black devils were going to savage me.' He had a cultivated,

14

pleasant voice, which somehow suggested it could hold a hint of laughter, even when he appeared to be serious, but he was far from laughing at that moment; he was scowling at the dogs, who, pink tongues lolling, continued to eye him suspiciously. Damaris saw a lean, brown face, with an aquiline nose, surmounted by a thick thatch of black hair.

'They wouldn't really bite, but you see you're trespassing,' she told him.

'Oh, nonsense.' He rose to his feet with a quick, lithe movement, and looked down at her. She realised that he was considerably taller than she was, about six feet, her grandfather's height. The shale shifted under his feet, and as he sought securer footing, the dogs growled.

'You're well guarded,' he remarked, 'but may I point out that all these cliffs belong to the National Trust?'

'Not those below the Ravenscrag land,' she told him, 'and nobody ever comes here, there's no proper path and the beach is mostly slate. Didn't you see the warning notices?'

He laughed; his teeth were very white in his brown face. Bronze too were his exposed arms and legs, on which she noticed several scratches. He held himself with an arrogant, slightly reckless air, which was reflected in his voice, as he said:

'I never take any notice of warning notices. I regard them as a challenge.'

'That's not very wise round here,' she returned. 'These cliffs really are dangerous—the rock crumbles.'

He turned to look back at the grey rampart behind them, its bastions interspersed with falls of scree, over which gulls and birds of prey were circling.

'So I see, but how did you get here?'

His eyes swept over her, and she was surprised to see that they were a vivid blue, contrasting with his black brows, and fringed with long black lashes. He took in her slight figure, bare of arm and leg, the black shift, the bronze curls tangled about her small face. Finally his glance met hers and held. She became conscious of her scanty garb, her bare feet—she had abandoned her sandals—and deep within her something stirred, the first awareness of her womanhood.

'Perhaps you live here?' he went on. 'You're a sea nymph—what did the ancients call them—nereids; only a nereid or a sea witch could have such strange eyes.'

His voice was low, gently teasing, his eyes intent, his gaze magnetic. Colour rose to stain her face, and with an effort she turned her head away, to look towards the sea.

'I live at Ravenscrag,' she told him, 'and there is a way down the cliff, though only Granddad and I know it.'

'And your grandfather, is he here with you?' he asked, looking past her as if expecting to see him.

She shook her head. 'No. He's dead,' she said flatly.

'I'm sorry,' he said gently. 'Did you live with him?'

'Yes, he was all I had.'

'Poor little kid!'

'I'm not a kid,' she said indignantly, then lifting her small chin, she added proudly, 'I'm Damaris Treherne.'

The stranger stared at her incredulously.

'Damaris Treherne? You're kidding.'

'I'm not. Sir Hugh Treherne was my grandfather, but of course you're only a visitor, you won't have heard of the Trehernes.'

He gave a low whistle, and his eyes raked her from bronze curls to bare feet with open amusement. 'Damaris Treherne—well, I'll be damned!' Seeing her surprised expression, he went on, 'Sorry, I didn't mean to be rude. I have heard of the Trehernes; at the farm where I'm staying everyone has been talking about Sir Hugh's sudden death, but from what they said I understood Miss Treherne was grown up and very much the lady of the Manor.'

'I am grown up,' she flashed at him indignantly. 'I'm eighteen.' He looked astonished. 'This frock was run up in a hurry—I—I wanted something black, but I look very different when I'm properly dressed.' She drew herself with a quaint assumption of dignity that her appearance did nothing to support. 'Naturally I don't put on my best clothes to take the dogs for a run on the beach.'

'Naturally,' he agreed, his eyes crinkling with laughter. 'Again I apologise. I'm sure you look most impressive when you're—er—dressed up.'

She did not like his tone, suspecting he was mocking her. Did he still not believe her? He continued to study her with an amusement that Damaris was beginning to resent. While she was searching her mind for a scathing remark that would put him in his place, for all said and done he was intruding upon her territory. Tris gave a whimper. He thought he had been sitting long enough. His mistress seemed to have forgotten her dogs, and an inquisitive jackdaw, tantalisingly near, was taunting him, but both animals were too well trained to move without permission.

'Up, dogs, off you go,' Damaris ordered, not sorry for a diversion. Sol was away like an arrow, a black streak through the sunlight, while the jackdaw rose with a squawk, but Tris, more conscientious, lingered, distrustfully eyeing the stranger.

'Friend, Tris,' Damaris told him.

'Here, boy,' the man said encouragingly, holding out his hand. Tris sniffed it doubtfully; wise in doggy ways, the stranger neither advanced nor retreated. Tris continued to sniff, his survey including shoes and legs, then, satisfied, he slowly moved his tail, which began to wag with increasing acceleration. Then he licked the brown fingers extended towards him.

'What do you call him? Tris? That's a funny name for a dog,' he remarked.

'It's short for Tristan, and his mate's called Isolde,' she told him, as Tris ran after his wife. 'Tristram or Tristan was one of Arthur's knights, and he was in love with Iseult, or Isolde as Wagner calls her ...'

'Yes, I know the tale,' he interrupted her. 'This place teems with Arthurian legends. Tintagel, wasn't it, where the wronged King Mark had his castle,' and he quoted, ' "half in the sea and half on land a crown of towers". That's a place I must visit.'

'There aren't any towers left,' she said, half charmed, half antagonised by her companion. She was about to ask him what his name was, when she noticed a red scratch on his arm was bleeding.

'You're hurt, there's blood on your arm.'

He looked at it indifferently, and began to dab it with his handkerchief.

Damaris watched this proceeding with disfavour.

'You ought to have it attended to properly,' she said anxiously. 'I'll show you the way up and then Carrie can put a plaster on it.'

'It's nothing,' he said carelessly. 'I'll bathe it in sea water, that's a good disinfectant, you know.'

'Yes, but it'll make it smart.'

He knelt by a hollow in the rocks filled with the residue of the tide, and his subsequent grimace proved the truth of her warning.

'Who's Carrie?' he asked, intent upon his task.

'Miss Carew, my governess, I always call her Carrie.'

His eyes flashed up to her. 'Good grief, how Victorian! Why didn't you go to school?'

'Well—er—there isn't a suitable one near here and Granddad didn't want to part with me; besides, he— he didn't approve of modern young people. He said they'd no morals, manners or sense of responsibility.' She brought out this indictment with an odd mixture of primness and assurance. Evidently she firmly believed in its truth. The man watching her sat back on his heels, while the picture of her girlhood became clear to him. She had been brought up like a little nun.

'Your grandfather must have been a regular old die-hard,' he said a trifle grimly, 'but he'd no right to let you become a complete ignoramus.'

'But I'm not!' Again she was indignant. 'Carrie's a very good teacher, and she's got all sorts of degrees and things. She says I'm quite bright at history, languages and English, but not maths, that's my weak point.'

'Women are rarely mathematicians,' he said drily. 'Figures involve logic, and what female is logical? But I wasn't doubting your academic qualifications, my child. What I meant was, you probably know a great deal more about the ancient Britons than modern homo sapiens.'

'I know that's Latin,' she told him triumphantly, 'and means the human species.'

'Of which I'm a specimen, a modern specimen, and as such I represent the decadent age from which you've been so carefully excluded.'

She flushed, wondering if she had been rude, or whether he were laughing at her.

'I didn't mean anything personal . . .' she faltered.

'I'm sure you didn't. Well, do I give you the impression that I've no morals, sense of responsibility or manners?' He stood up, folded his arms and regarded her quizzically, inviting her inspection.

She made a fluttering gesture with her hands. 'How can I tell? I've only known you five minutes, and I don't think you're very polite to try to twist everything I say.'

He laughed goodhumouredly. The waif had spirit!

'And you've never wanted to rebel against this isolation?'

'Why should I? We were very happy together, Granddad and I. We didn't want anybody except each other.'

Her lips trembled and she turned away her head so

that he should not see the tears that had risen to her eyes.

He said gently, 'And now—what are you going to do with your life?'

'Nothing. I'm waiting for Cousin Mark.'

'Indeed?' he raised his eyebrows. 'And who is Cousin Mark?'

'Mark Treherne, the next baronet. He's in South America and I'm engaged to him.'

'You're what?' he exclaimed.

'Engaged to be married to him. It was in Granddad's will.'

'Good lord!' He looked so taken aback that she stared at him in surprise. 'But surely . . .' he began, then checked himself. He gave her a lop-sided smile. 'You've met your fiancé, of course?' His expression was enigmatical.

She shook her head. 'No, never.'

'You mean to tell me you've let yourself become engaged to a total stranger?'

'He's not a stranger, he's family,' she said defensively, defining Mark as she had defined him to Helen. 'Someone who has the same name as mine can't be called a stranger.' She looked at him uncertainly. 'But you wouldn't understand, Granddad said people today didn't believe in traditions.'

He smiled again, and this time the smile was wholly charming.

'Not to that extent,' he said lightly. 'Anyway, one doesn't expect a nereid to contract a human betrothal. Suppose you tell me all about it?'

He indicated a ledge of rock and sat down. Somewhat warily she seated herself beside him, carefully pulling her scanty dress over her knees. She was eager to tell her story, for except for a disapproving Helen she had had no confidant during the sad days following her bereavement. It was a relief to pour it all out, even though her companion has not so far been very sympathetic. She concluded her recital by saying, 'So you see it's my duty to marry Cousin Mark.'

'How nice for him,' he commented wryly. 'But good grief, child, it's an impossible situation. You've spent all your life mewed up here without meeting anyone of your own age. You're completely ignorant of the world and its ways. You've no experience of men, or women, while this Mark ... do you know how old he is?'

'Not exactly, but I think he's middle-aged.'

'Oh!' He looked disconcerted, then he went on vehemently, 'Don't you see, he'd be a skunk if he took advantage of your ignorance and innocence to hold you to this ridiculous bargain to strengthen his title to the estate.'

She said with dignity, 'It's not in the least ridiculous, and I like older men.'

'But, child, you haven't lived at all, and he may have ... er ... lived too much.'

She looked puzzled. 'I don't know what you mean, and of course Granddad knew what was best for me. He told me Cousin Mark would look after me.'

Her companion moved impatiently. 'So you're prepared to be handed on from one old man to another?' he asked with exasperation. 'And you shouldn't need looking after if you're really grown up. An adult woman stands on her own feet.'

Involuntarily they both glanced down at her slim, bare feet; they looked fragile and babyish, the brown toes curling amid the grey sand, and oddly appealing, but their appearance seemed to annoy him.

'Don't you wear shoes?' he asked curtly. 'You could cut your feet on all this slate.'

'Oh, yes, my sandals are over there,' she waved a vague hand, 'but if I don't marry Cousin Mark, I'll have to leave Ravenscrag, and that would break my heart.'

'I suppose it hasn't occurred to you that your cousin might break your heart?' He spoke almost roughly.

The grey-green eyes with their specks of gold met his in a bewildered stare.

'Why should he?'

'Because he doesn't love you, and if he marries you only from a sense of duty, you haven't much hope of happiness.'

Her eyes widened in dismay. 'Why shouldn't he love me? Am I repulsive?'

'Far from it, but love doesn't come to order, and an arranged marriage can be hell.'

She smiled with a hint of mischief. 'Are you married?'

'God forbid! I like my freedom too well.'

'Then you can hardly be an authority on the subject,' she pointed out, 'you're a ... a ...' She cast about in her mind for the appropriate word to describe him, and her reading came to her aid, 'philanderer!' she said triumphantly.

He had much ado to conceal his amusement. He leaned back against the rock behind him and regarded her lazily through half shut eyes, a problem, he thought, for Cousin Mark, but one that might be rewarding to unravel, if he had the time and the patience, he himself was not a patient man. Something in his expression made Damaris faintly uneasy. She lowered her lids and turned away her head.

'Take my advice,' he said suddenly, 'forget all about this—er—elderly cousin, go out into the world and have some fun with youngsters of your own age, and fall in love with a long-haired boy, who's your equal in inexperience.'

There was a tinge of bitterness in his voice.

'But that means leaving Ravenscrag, and I don't think I'll ever fall in love. Cousin Mark will suit me very well, if he's kind.'

'Kind!' he was contemptuous. 'Is kindness all you want from a husband?'

'It's the most important thing,' she said sagely. 'I'm

hoping he'll be like Granddad and I can do all the little things for him that I did for my grandfather.'

'Fill his hot water bottle and warm his slippers?' Her companion picked up a stone and flung it against a rock with a gesture that was almost savage. 'Lord, what a kid you are! What you're suffering from is a father—or rather a grandfather complex.'

Never having heard of psycho-analysis, she looked blank, but his action had drawn her attention to the incoming tide.

'If we don't want a wetting, we'd better be going,' she said, rising to her feet. 'I'll show you the way up.'

She moved away to retrieve her sandals, and he followed the slight, graceful figure with a crease between his brows. Completely unawakened and unsophisticated, with only her devotion to her grandfather's memory to guide her, she was terribly vulnerable, and he did not like to contemplate her ultimate fate. She was a nice child, an amusing child, with intriguing possibilities, but still a child.

Damaris whistled to the dogs, who came galloping up to her in response to her summons, and in silence led the way up the almost imperceptible path. It led in rough hewn steps up behind a slab of rock, huge as a truck and much the same oblong shape, which masked it from any but a keenly observant eye. On top of the rock, where sea-pinks were massed, the path vanished into a jungle of bracken and bushes of honeysuckle, which she pushed aside, to reveal the narrow track; beyond it climbed again, a narrow shelf, zig-zagging across the scree fallen from the heights above. Nimbly she led the way, with the sureness of long familiarity, while the dogs gingerly followed in their wake, her mind in a whirl of conjecture.

The stranger had shaken her confidence in her future. Was it possible that she did regard Mark as a sort of grandfather, who would take over where Sir Hugh had left off, and he might prove to be something very different? Perhaps he might be like the young man who had literally dropped at her feet, and thought, as he appeared to do, that she was still a child in the care of a governess and unfit to be mistress of Ravenscrag? Then she recalled that her companion belonged to the generation against which she had been warned, and would have a completely different set of values. He would have no idea of what the Manor and its traditions meant to her and Cousin Mark, a shared inheritance that would be a bond between them. Mark, too, would have no thought of going against her grandfather's wishes, and would understand that she could not contemplate doing so. As for the suggestion that she should go out into the whirl of modern young society, she shrank from it with fear and abhorrence, feeling that among her own age group she would be a fish out of water, far better to submit to her cousin, and hope that he would cherish her as Sir Hugh had done.

The last part of the ascent wound up between two precipitous crags, and then they emerged on to the short turf at the cliffs' edge. Below them the water was churning over the place where they had recently been sitting, and the sea stretched, glittering in the sunlight to the horizon across which Mark would soon be coming to claim her.

'The house is down there,' she said, pointing across the two fields from which the hay had been lifted, that lay between them and a clump of trees in a hollow. The dogs, glad to have completed their climbing feat, were already careering towards it.

'You'll come back with me?'

'No, thank you, I've left my car up at the farm and I'm not in a fit state to meet your—er—governess.' He glanced ruefully at his torn shirt.

'Oh, Carrie won't mind,' she urged, 'she's used to me coming in looking a wreck, and she'll put something on your scratches.'

'But I'm not you,' he pointed out, 'and when I pay

calls I like to be suitably dressed for the occasion. I gather the Manor is something of a stately home and should be treated with respect.'

She sighed. 'Not so stately nowadays, it's getting a bit shabby.' Sir Hugh in his old age had not bothered with refurnishing, preferring the old familiar surroundings.

'Indeed? Then the new owner will have plenty to occupy him.'

'I hope he won't alter anything,' Damaris said anxiously. 'I'd hate that.'

'Change is the law of life,' he told her. 'You'll change too, and you can't expect a new broom not to sweep clean.' Again the note of derision she so disliked. 'These hayfields,' he went on, 'are dirty. They need ploughing out and re-seeding.' He was looking about him with a speculative eye, and with his attention diverted, she in her turn studied him. Evidently he knew something about agriculture—a farmer, perhaps? She saw now that he was not as young as she had supposed from his unconventional clothes. There were tiny lines at the corners of his well-shaped mouth and keen blue eyes. He was burned very dark by a stronger sun than that of Britain, possibly he had been abroad. She decided he was at least twenty-five, which to her was advanced maturity. His eyes came back to her and met her interested gaze.

'What is it?' he asked.

She blushed and hung her head. 'Nothing. I was wondering exactly how old Cousin Mark is,' she lied.

'Afraid he'll be in his dotage?'

'Don't be absurd, but he must be well over thirty,' she said seriously. 'That's getting on, isn't it?'

He laughed. 'Quite a Methuselah,' he agreed, 'but I can assure you that at thirty, or even forty, men are still quite vigorous.'

'Granddad was vigorous at seventy,' she told him.

'Not quite what I meant.' He reached out and took hold of her chin, raising her face. 'Look at me,' he commanded.

Drawn by some magnetism that she could not resist, she slowly raised her long black lashes to meet his intent blue gaze. His eyes were narrower than hers, and surrounded by lashes as thick and long as her own. Something in their close regard disturbed her, her heart quickened its beat, and she felt the blood rise to her cheeks.

'You've got witch's eyes,' he murmured. 'You'll do some damage with them before you've done. I'm beginning to envy Cousin Mark.'

He bent his head and deliberately kissed her mouth. It was a very gentle kiss, but even so an electric current pulsed through her, to be succeeded by swift reaction, a virginal sense of outrage. She pushed his hand away, and her eyes blazed.

'What ... what did you do that for?' she gasped.

He shrugged his broad shoulders and an impish gleam came into his eyes.

'An impulse. Perhaps I wanted to show you that there are other men in the world besides grandfathers.'

Stung, she cried, 'If there are, I don't want to know them!'

He smiled mockingly. 'Then I'll be off. Goodbye, nereid.'

He went from her, loping over the meadow, while she stood watching his tall figure recede, bewildered by the turmoil of her emotions evoked by that unsought kiss. It was not until he was climbing the opposite slope, a mere dot on the expanse of green fields and grey outcrop, that she realised he had not told her his name. It was of no importance, she thought, as she started homeward, she would not see him again, and tried to persuade herself that she was glad it should be so. He did not fit into her enclosed little world, his words—and actions—had been uncomfortably disturbing. She decided that she had not liked him. She did not mention the encounter to Helen, who, she felt vaguely, would disapprove. She had always been forbidden to talk to strangers; but that night she dreamed she was with him again on the rocks of the seashore; it was a wild and stormy day and she was terrified of the raging sea, until he took her into his arms, saying:

'Don't be frightened, you'll always be safe with me.'

Which was, of course, quite absurd. Sir Hugh and Cousin Mark were her natural protectors, never that stranger.

Some time later Mr. Preston came again to visit Ravenscrag and he brought disturbing news. He had been in touch with Sir Mark Treherne and between them they had decided that Damaris should spend a year abroad at a finishing school in Switzerland. As co-trustee, the solicitor had approved the idea; it was what the child needed, young companionship and education in the social graces.

Helen Carew, who also thoroughly approved of the plan, remarked a little caustically, 'She's to be groomed for the position she'll one day fill?' and cocked an enquiring eyebrow at the dry little man, but Mr. Preston refused to be drawn.

'Possibly,' he said non-committally.

Damaris received the news with consternation and open rebellion.

'I won't go,' she protested, 'and you can't make me go. I'd be miserable among a lot of strange girls.'

'Of course you'll go,' Helen returned. 'It's an excellent plan. Teach you to stand on your own feet.'

Damaris glanced down at her neatly shod feet and saw in their place bare toes and recalled a lazy, mocking voice saying, 'An adult woman stands on her own feet.' She looked uncertainly towards Mr. Preston, who was watching her anxiously.

'I suppose Cousin Mark thinks I'm too ignorant and raw to marry me as I am,' she said angrily.

'You're still very young,' the solicitor said soothingly.

'There's plenty of time before you make any irrevocable decision——' (But I've made mine, she thought, there wasn't any choice). 'You'll find the training this establishment offers you very helpful in the future.'

He held out to her an elegantly designed booklet setting forth the innumerable advantages to be gained from a course at Madame Le Brun's Académie pour Jeunes Filles.

Damaris took it and threw it on the floor.

'If I was good enough for Granddad, I'm good enough for Cousin Mark without frills,' she told him scornfully. She was hurt and angry that her fiancé had not communicated with her himself, but had left all arrangements to the solicitor, who did not even seem to know where he was.

Mr. Preston sighed. The Treherne temper was proverbial in the annals of Preston, Poldark and Preston, who had managed the affairs of Ravenscrag for several generations.

Helen picked up the booklet. 'Don't be so silly, Damaris,' she said severely, 'you need to learn how to dress and entertain. This place,' she touched the syllabus she held, 'is rather more than a school. They will prepare you for the life a titled lady has to lead. Sir Mark won't be a recluse like your grandfather. You'll have to give dinner parties, cocktail parties, perhaps even house parties, open bazaars, sit on committees ...' She was deliberately listing all the functions she could recall in the hope of intimidating her obstreperous charge.

'Oh, please,' Damaris quailed. 'How awful!' she said.

'A year abroad will give you the confidence you need,' Helen urged. Privately she thought Sir Mark was seeking a way out. Twelve months in Switzerland would delay the issue, and if Damaris made friends who had attractive brothers, she might at the end of that time be as anxious to repudiate the engagement as he was. He could retire gracefully with honour unsullied. He had not suggested meeting the girl, which implied that he was not exactly enthusiastic about the union. Damaris felt humiliated by this neglect. Surely Cousin Mark might have made an effort to see her before banishing her abroad, to give her the comfort and reassurance he must surely realise that she needed? The dreadful thought occurred to her that perhaps he simply did not care. Her pride awoke; she would make him care, she would come back so poised and elegant he would have to acknowledge she would make an ideal Lady Treherne.

'Very well, I'll go,' she conceded. 'I'll make him proud of me.'

'That's the spirit!' Helen approved.

Damaris gave a wail. 'But the dogs! I'd forgotten them. They'll be unhappy at Ravenscrag without me. They'll be shut up most of the time, and they're not used to it. I can't leave them.'

'I'll take them,' Helen said heroically, for though she was fond of Tris and Sol, two large labradors would create a bit of a problem on her friend's limited premises.

'Oh, would you, Carrie, and give them a walk every day?'

'Yes,' Helen promised valiantly. 'You can be quite easy about them.'

'Thank you,' Damaris said faintly, realising there was now no retreat.

'Mrs. Garth is looking after the Manor, and Sir Mark is installing a bailiff until he takes over himself,' Mr. Preston announced.

Damaris did not like that 'takes over'. She remembered uneasily the encounter on the beach and the stranger's remark about 'change'. However, there was nothing she could do about it, even if she stayed.

'Mary and I will always make you very welcome if ever you want a home,' Helen told her, thinking the need might well arise. Mary Brooke was her friend with whom she was going to live.

'Thank you, but I shan't,' Damaris told her, with a touch of defiance. 'Ravenscrag is my home and I'll be coming back to marry Cousin Mark.'

'Yes, of course,' Helen agreed hastily, and exchanged glances with the solicitor. Both doubted the validity of that statement.

But Damaris had no doubts whatever about her ultimate destiny, and it was in the firm conviction that she would return to be Cousin Mark's bride that she set forth for Switzerland, without however having even glimpsed her future husband.

CHAPTER TWO

MADAME LE BRUN claimed descent from the Madame Vigée Le Burn who had been a court painter to Marie Antoinette. The truth of this claim was open to question, but no one could deny that she had the same name, and the pedigree, fictitious or otherwise, struck just the right note of distinction necessary for the Head of her extremely exclusive Académie pour Jeunes Filles. This was situated in what had once been a convent on the shores of Lac Léman not far from Geneva. She catered for the daughters of moneyed people, who wished their offspring to be groomed for their entry into the world of wealth and fashion, and her pupils were all young ladies in their late teens undergoing the process of 'finishing'.

The curriculum laid emphasis on languages, deportment, dancing and those sports a knowledge of which would be a social advantage. The girls wore during the day, simple skirts and blouses, when they were not in sports clothes, but all dressed for a formal dinner in the evening, as part of their training in drawing-room etiquette; nor was the more practical side neglected. The girls learned how to make up a menu, and such things as the correct wines to serve with each course, and of course the order of precedence in high society.

Damaris Treherne was met at the airport by the school car complete with attendant governess. She descended from the aircraft clutching her hand luggage in a maze of apprehension. Her heavier luggage, which included an astonishing number of outfits as laid down in the list Helen Carew had been sent, had gone on ahead. Damaris felt shy and bewildered and had not altogether enjoyed her first taste of air travel, which

31

had made her feel queasy. The mistress who had come to receive her eyed her anxiously. The account Madame Le Brun had been given of Damaris' antecedents had led her to expect a hoyden, but the girl seemed quiet and well-mannered, and the woman was greatly relieved. There would be no difficulties with this one.

It was a still evening in early autumn. The term began at the end of September, after a long summer break; a rising mist hung over the lake, and the tops of the long range of mountains were veiled. The car sped along a well-metalled road and Damaris caught glimpses of deep-eaved chalet-type houses, the window boxes and gardens still ablaze with flowers.

'It is pretty, is it not?' the governess asked in French, and was pleased when Damaris tried to answer in the same tongue. Her accent left something to be desired, but she obviously knew the language and was not afraid to try to speak it.

Upon arrival, she was shown into a cell-like bedroom; in fact it had been a nun's cell, which was adequately, if not luxuriously furnished with bright curtains and cover on the divan-style bed. The furniture was light painted wicker, the wardrobe built into the thickness of the wall—and the walls of the old building were very thick—had a long glass in its door. Her luggage had arrived and stood on the rack at the foot of the bed.

'We dine at seven of the clock,' the governess told her, a statement that surprised Damaris, whose ideas of school were founded upon Charlotte Brontë's books. 'You will change, of course. I will send Céleste to show you round. Madame will see you in her study after dinner.' She left the apprehensive newcomer alone with the prospect of facing a table full of strange faces; she began to unpack her cases with a sinking heart, dreading the ordeal before her. Strange girls, girls of her own age were an unknown quantity, never having mingled with any before.

A tap on the door and a young woman came in. She was already dressed for the meal in a pink chiffon frock, her dark hair curled elaborately upon her head, and looked so adult that Damaris thought she must be another mistress.

'*Bonsoir, petite*,' she said gaily. 'Do not look as though you expect to be eaten! I am Céleste de Valmond and I hope that we shall be friends.'

'I hope so too,' Damaris agreed, liking what she saw of Céleste.

'You have the frock most simple?' Céleste went on. 'Look at me—this dress is like the little girl in the pantomime, but Madame will have it so; it is different, I assure you, when I go home, then I wear the trouser suits, the plunging neckline—ah!' as Damaris shook out a simple white shift, 'that will please Madame, you make the good impression, yes? Put that one on!'

The ordeal was no longer so terrible under Céleste's sheltering wing. They soon became firm friends. Throughout all the bewilderment of that first term, Céleste was Damaris' shield and bulwark. The attraction between the sparkling French girl and the subdued English one was that of opposites, for Damaris did anything but sparkle during her preliminary weeks, though Céleste hinted that a time would come when her protégée would surprise them all.

'She has not *les yeux de diable* for nothing,' she declared. 'Wait, *mes enfants*, until she has found her feet.'

Always this emphasis upon feet, Damaris thought drily, and wondered fleetingly what had happened to the man who had first drawn her attention to hers, and had also said that she had witch's eyes. Nobody in the neighbourhood of Ravenscrag seemed to know anything about him, though she had made discreet enquiries. Sometimes she wondered if she had dreamed the whole episode.

Her companions were a mixed bag of varying nationalities, including North Americans. The Academy catered for rich girls and preferably the well-born, but in the changing values of the modern world, it was not the aristocrats who had the most money. Madame sought to leaven the lump of *nouveaux riches* with a few students from old families whom she accepted at reduced fees for the sake of their names. One of these was Céleste de Valmond, whose father owned a dilapidated château in the Haute Savoie, and possessed a title which he no longer used, though Madame made frequent references to the Comte de Valmond. Céleste, who understood her perfectly, shrugged as she said to Damaris, 'My price of admission.' But someone is paying full terms for me, the Cornish girl thought. Cousin Mark and/or Mr. Preston? It seemed to her a little unnecessary, but it carried an obligation to do her best. This was not difficult; she was sufficiently well grounded by Miss Carew to find the lessons easy, and she was a good sportswoman, but the social aspect was another matter.

A segregated collection of high-spirited young women, and the students were all nearly women, tends to intense concentration upon the opposite sex, an attitude which puzzled and shocked Damaris who in this connection was still a child. Her reading, supervised by a succession of governesses, had been mainly classical and did not include romances or magazines. There had been no television at Ravenscrag and only rare visits to the cinema. Love, when she thought about it, was represented by lifelong union, or, if illicit, tragedy. The easy susceptibility of her comrades seemed so trivial, their more daring utterances insincere, their whispering and giggling silly. One sophisticated Parisienne, Odette Lamont, boasted openly of violent episodes during the summer break, wherein she had given all to prevent an ardent lover from committing suicide, a revelation which impressed the girls, as she meant it to do, but was in fact a fabrication. Céleste was not deceived.

'That one has the imagination very great,' she told Damaris. 'It is most unlikely that her *beau* did more than kiss her behind a door.'

'Then why tell lies?' Damaris asked bluntly.

Céleste shrugged her shoulders. 'To gull the silly ones and make of herself the heroine of a romance. We read much about the free life, but Papa Lamont is not one to let Odette sample it. I have met him.'

'It's all beyond me,' Damaris said. It was the time before dinner. Céleste had changed early and had come into her room while she completed her own toilet. She had not confided to her friend the fact of her own engagement. For one thing she had no ring to confirm it, nor did she receive any letters from her fiancé, and shrewdly suspected her comrades, even Céleste, would think she was inventing her betrothal to boost her own importance, in the same way that Odette made up her fairy-tales.

'What would you?' Céleste was tolerant. 'The romance is what we all yearn for. Men are the most exciting thing in life, and to be kissed by a handsome boy. Oh, la, la!' She rolled her brown eyes expressively.

Damaris opened her eyes wide.

'I don't think being kissed behind a door can be nearly as thrilling as a gallop across country.'

'Ah, but you are the little savage, and you lived always with that old *grandpère*, of which you tell me. He is very strict, *n'est-ce pas*? It is that you have never been kissed?'

'Oh, yes, I've been kissed,' Damaris admitted in what she hoped was a nonchalant tone. 'I didn't think it was anything to make a song about,' but she coloured as she made the confession, recalling her sensations on the cliff top, and went on hastily, 'All this playing with love, it ... it's rather cheap.' Her lip curled fastidiously.

'You are waiting for *la grande passion*?' Céleste

asked seriously. 'But it does not come to all of us, which perhaps is as well, for it seems it can be most uncomfortable. Me, I shall have to settle for some ordinary individual who can give me a suitable competence, for we are not well off.'

Céleste was French and practical.

'But you have your dream man?' Damaris suggested, reflecting that she herself was making a marriage very much of convenience. 'How do you imagine your ideal lover?'

Céleste looked pensive. 'Tall and fair,' she began, 'not very young. I would prefer a man of the world, who has had affairs with many women.' Damaris gasped, and Céleste giggled. 'So that he would know his way about,' she explained, 'but of course he would never have truly loved until he met me.' Her eyes grew dreamy. 'He would seem hard and cold outside, perhaps even a little cruel, but underneath would be hidden fire, you understand, which would ignite only for me. He would sweep me off my feet, he would be crazy about me, and I ... I should be aloof at first, but in the end...' Her voice trailed off and she sat motionless, absorbed in her erotic dream.

'Sounds fine,' Damaris said prosaically, 'but are you likely to meet your heart-throb?'

Céleste recalled herself and laughed ruefully. 'Not one little hope, *chérie*, I don't suppose there is such a man outside the pages of a book—but you, haven't you an ideal lover?'

'Oh yes,' Damaris was quite ready to play Céleste's game. 'Mine would be tall too, but dark, with bright blue eyes. He's burnt by the sun, and he has a profile like an eagle. He's got a funny sort of smile that does things to...' She stopped, confused, aware she was trying to describe the man she had encountered at the foot of the cliff.

'You're blushing!' Céleste exclaimed. 'Can it be that you've met him?'

'Perhaps I have,' Damaris admitted, not unwilling to score over her more sophisticated friend, 'which is more than you've done.'

'And he admired you? He fell at your feet?' Céleste asked eagerly.

'He fell at my feet,' Damaris said, laughing, 'but he didn't admire me, he thought I was a mere child.'

'How sad! But all that will be changed when he sees you again. You do not look like a child now.'

Damaris turned to study her image in the long glass. She wore a long green dress, simple and clinging, one of the two Helen had ordered for her from a well-known dress house. Her hair had been cut by a Geneva hairdresser—Madame encouraged such extravagances—and curled becomingly round her heart-shaped face. Under Céleste's tutelage she had skilfully applied the modicule of make-up allowed by the school. The reflection that looked back at her was sophisticated, even alluring, but all this had been achieved not to impress any fascinating stranger, but her elderly Cousin Mark.

'No,' she agreed, 'I don't look like a child, but I shan't meet that man again.'

The Christmas break was a short one. Helen Carew wrote to say that it would not be worth while to come home, by which she meant her own place in Boscastle. Ravenscrag was in the throes of being redecorated, information that angered Damaris; surely she should have been consulted about that? Sir Mark and Mr. Preston still seemed to consider that she was too juvenile to have a say in the future appearance of her home. She was to spend the holiday at the Academy, where several other girls were also staying, an American and two French girls whose parents were abroad, but not Céleste, who was going back to Valmond.

'I wish that I could ask you to accompany me,' her friend told her, 'but at Noel it is impossible. Maman invites all the family, uncles, aunts and children, it will not be very amusing. I hope that you will come at Easter, when we shall be on our own.'

Damaris thanked her, but was determined Easter would find her at Ravenscrag.

'I will bring you back a box of *marrons glacés*,' Céleste promised. 'Savoy is famed for its *marrons glacés*, and they are most delectable.'

But the prospect of *marrons glacés*, however delectable, could not compensate for exile. Damaris was homesick, thinking wistfully of the Manor as it had always been during the Christmas season, with its piled log fires—the Academy had central heating—the holly decorations that she always put up, and Tris and Sol lying on the hearthrug. She longed for the soft mist and rain driving in from the Atlantic, the sound of breakers and the joy of finding the first snowdrops and aconites in the garden. The country round Geneva sparkled under a mantle of snow, the mountains were dramatic against a background of blue sky, while the town was thronged with tourists on their way to the ski-slopes, but it was all alien to the Cornish girl, sighing for home.

Helen sent her a handsome hand-woven poncho from the shop that she now ran in conjunction with Mary Brooke, and snapshots of the dogs and Mary's little boy, David. In her accompanying letter she said that she had met Mrs. Garth, the housekeeper from Ravenscrag, who had asked after her. Sir Mark had come and gone; he seemed a nice gentleman—Mrs. Garth's words, she herself had not seen him. Mr. Preston sent her a card, a snow scene—as if we didn't have more than enough of that here! Damaris thought, who would have appreciated something typically Cornish. He enclosed a generous cheque for expenses. Madame Le Brun gave her four stranded boarders' bath salts and scent, and they gave each other trifles from the souvenir shops.

On Christmas Day, after going to church, Damaris

was surprised to find in her room a large bunch of cellophane-wrapped flowers, carnations and roses, as well as a small parcel. The flowers had been delivered from a local florist and bore a card inscribed, 'Compliments de Noel.' Céleste? she wondered. But Céleste could not afford such an expensive gesture. She opened the parcel, also sent from a shop in Geneva. It contained a silver bracelet hung with charms, and rummaging among the wrappings she came upon a slip of pasteboard, on which was written, 'Hope this will bring you luck. M.' M.? Could it be Mark? Had he at last acknowledged her existence? The writing looked like a man's, thick and black, and she knew no other male, except Mr. Preston, whose name was Albert. She picked up the bracelet and one by one examined the charms—a silver shoe, a churn, a St. Christopher, a windmill, a pram and a penny-farthing cycle, the sort of thing that might appeal to a very young schoolgirl. Mark was still waiting for her to grow up. Despondently she laid it down on her dressing-table. She supposed that she should be gratified that he had remembered her at all, though surely in the circumstances it would have been more appropriate to send her a ring. She would have liked that, a ring could have been displayed to the other girls with the news that she was an engaged girl, and she would have enjoyed the consequent rise in status. Her thinking was still very juvenile.

One of the maids knocked and came into the room. Mademoiselle had received her gifts, but yes? They had been sent up by hand from the town. So the flowers also were from Mark Treherne. The maid was plainly curious, suspecting an admirer.

'They're from a cousin in England,' Damaris told her and the girl looked disappointed. Her colleagues had seen the flowers being delivered and accepted her explanation with their own embellishments.

'A cousin can also be a *beau*,' one of the French girls

39

said. 'Is he in love with you?'

'My folks think first cousins shouldn't marry,' the American said sourly.

'It often happens in France,' from the other French girl. 'I wish I had a cousin to send me bouquets.'

Damaris did not bother to explain the exact relationship; a second cousin was still a kinsman, though not so close. Even so, and without a ring, she found that her prestige had soared.

Céleste returned with the promised *marron glacé*, complaining that she had spent a dull holiday with a house full of children and no eligible man.

'Don't you like children?' asked Damaris, who did.

Céleste shrugged. 'Me, I want the romance; the nursery comes afterwards.'

She pounced at once upon the charm bracelet, which Damaris was wearing.

'From him?' she demanded.

'A him, yes, but not the one you mean.'

'Damaris, you are a dark horse; how many young men have you got in tow?'

'None. This is from a relation.'

'How dull!' Céleste lost interest in the trinket. She brought an invitation from Madame de Valmond to spend the Easter holidays at the Château, which had to be referred to her guardians, though Damaris, now nineteen, thought the formality unnecessary, but she was still uncertain about her financial position, the allowance Mr. Preston sent her she assumed was from her own income, and when she returned he would permit her to have control of it. Meanwhile, Madame Le Brun would not allow the visit without referring to him. She had hoped very much that he would suggest a return to Cornwall, for surely it was time she met Cousin Mark, who seemed unflatteringly incurious about his prospective bride, but when Mr. Preston wrote, it was approving the visit to Valmond. It seemed that her year abroad was to be a year without remittance, and since she had agreed to it, she must endure it, but she secretly felt that she had acquired quite sufficient polish to satisfy Cousin Mark's requirements without wasting further money upon her social education. However, as there would be only one more term to endure to complete the year, it was not worth a rebellion.

Nevertheless her spirits rose when one bright spring day the dreary winter term behind them, she set out in the hired car with Céleste for Savoy. The lake looked like blue silk in the sunlight, and amid the snow-clad peaks unobscured by cloud, the mass of Mont Blanc was clearly visible. They crossed the frontier with a perfunctory glance at their cases by the Customs officers, and the road began to rise, passing through Thonon, a small market town by the lakeside, through smiling meadows and higher into overhanging woods, split by grey, formidable crags. Chalet-type farm houses with deep-eaved roofs clung to the hillsides, and below the road, the river swollen with melted snows, rushed foaming through deep gorges.

The Château de Valmond from the outside was a building out of a fairy-tale, its front flanked by round towers, each with its pepper-pot pointed pinnacle. It stood on a slight eminence surrounded by forest land, and below it the village nestled in a cleared space along the banks of the river. Damaris exclaimed with delight at sight of it, but Céleste shrugged her shoulders.

'I daresay it looks picturesque, but inside it's draughty and uncomfortable. Me, I am all for the new buildings of glass and concrete, but at least we have modern plumbing.'

The car ascended the steep road to the Château and pulled up on a wide gravel sweep in front of it. The remains of a formal garden was terraced in descending tiers beyond the drive; the house faced the valley up which they had come, with a superb view down its length, behind it the woods swept up to the skyline.

Damaris got out of the car and drank in the pine-scented air. The ponderous front door was open, and Madame de Valmond came out to greet them. She was a tiny woman, whose black hair was streaked with grey above her aquiline face, and despite her lack of inches, she expressed dignity in every line. Beside her stalked two enormous Afghan hounds, their yellow silky coats reflecting the sunlight, while their long-nosed faces expressed a dignity as great as that of their mistress.

'*Holà*, Napoléon, Joséphine!' Céleste exclaimed as the dogs came towards her waving their plumed tails. She caressed each hand, the animals receiving her attentions with stately aloofness. Very different, Damaris thought from the wild effusions Tris and Sol would have displayed to greet her if she had gone home; unconsciously she sighed.

'Is it that you greet the dogs before your *maman*?' Madame asked.

Céleste laughed and stooped to kiss her mother. Damaris saw that although Madame de Valmond made on a larger scale, they were both very much alike, having the same large brown eyes and dark hair. 'They reached me first,' Céleste explained. 'Maman, this is Damaris.'

'Ah, but she is *chic*,' Madame said, holding out her hand. 'Welcome, *ma chère*, to Valmond.' Immensely gratified, Damaris took the tiny hand and made the necessary polite remarks. To be called *chic* by a Frenchwoman was indeed a compliment. She had come a long way since her Ravenscrag days!

Her room was in one of the towers and was filled with massive old-fashioned furniture, including a large four-poster bed.

'I am sorry that it looks like an antique shop,' Céleste told her, 'but everything we have is old and shabby. The place looks like a morgue.'

'I think it's lovely,' Damaris said, and meant it.

'What a view!'

She went to the window—actually there were three in the semi-circular wall of the tower—and looked down the length of the valley, with the tree-clad hills rising on either side. Céleste was looking slightly embarrassed.

'I did not tell you before,' she spoke hesitantly. 'I didn't want Madame Le Brun to know, but ... well, the truth is ... we let accommodation during the summer ... it helps you see, and this big house,' she spread her hands, 'so much of it is empty most of the year.'

'Why not?' Damaris exclaimed. 'It's a thing lots of people do nowadays. Have you some guests here now? I hope they're nice people.'

Céleste brightened. 'Two Englishmen, Maman said, they are studying forestry. I haven't seen them, but I hope with you that they are nice.' She sighed. 'You know that my father is really the Comte de Valmond, but he has not used the title since the war. He says titles and paying guests do not go well together. Nevertheless, he is still very much of the *ancien régime*.'

Damaris sat down on the big square bed and laughed. 'It's all wonderful, Céleste, like a fairy-tale. I only hope that your guests fit into the picture.'

'At least,' Céleste said hopefully, 'they are males. Last summer we had some old women, tourists, who asked such boring questions. I only pray they are not bald and fat.'

'They'll hardly be that if they're forestry students,' Damaris pointed out.

'No,' Céleste agreed, 'and anything to do with forests sounds quite romantic.'

Romantic or otherwise, they were not to see their fellow guests until the evening, for it was their practice to take lunch with them and stay out all day. So for the midday meal served soon after their arrival, only the family were present.

Damaris found her host almost embarrassingly

courtly. With his pointed imperial, aristocratic features and spare upright figure, he looked as if he ought to be wearing a uniform or a silk and velvet suit, instead of the rather shabby tweed jacket that covered him. He was delighted to discover that she could speak French and most of the conversation was conducted in that language. She accepted with alacrity his offer to show her round the place after the meal, from which tour Céleste excused herself, being only too familiar with it. So, accompanied by the two hounds, Damaris and Monsieur de Valmond set forth. First the house itself, which was large, and many of the rooms unused.

'It is too difficult to heat,' he told her as they inspected the vast ballroom with its tarnished furnishings, then the library, with book-lined walls, and thence upstairs to the long gallery, that ran the length of the first floor, where pictures of departed de Valmonds stared down at them from wainscoted walls. Looking at them, Damaris was reminded of the family portraits in the dining room at Ravenscrag, a similar collection of dark-visaged men with their simpering ladies, though if anything the Trehernes were a more formidable-looking lot than the de Valmonds.

The hounds showed their approval when they went out of doors, frisking among the trees, their dignity temporarily forgotten and looking like huge woolly lambs. He showed her a walled kitchen garden, where an ancient Savoyard pottered about among the fruit and vegetables, which were the mainstay of the Château menus; the stables, which no longer housed horses, only an ancient Renault car.

'Once we possessed the finest bloodstock in the country,' Monsieur told her, sighing, 'but times change, and I can no longer ride.'

'It's a beautiful place,' Damaris said.

'It was in its time, but when I am gone it will have to be sold. Céleste does not care about it, she is all for life in the town, and I have no son to come after me.'

Damaris again thought of Ravenscrag where there had been no son to inherit. If only she had been a boy it would have come to her and she could have loved and tended it. A chill thought struck her; perhaps Mark, like Céleste, would not care for life on a country estate. But he could not sell it without her consent, and that she would never give, or so she surmised. She was still unsure of the exact situation.

Upon her return, she found Céleste going through her wardrobe. However straitened the family circumstances had become, her parents did not stint her. They might look shabby, but Céleste had plenty of clothes. She was deciding what she would wear to impress the foresters.

'So much depends upon the first sight,' she said. 'I wish to appear irresistible.'

'You may be wasting your efforts,' Damaris suggested, smiling. 'Very likely they'll be plain and very dull, and only interested in trees.'

Céleste's eyes gleamed. 'When they see me they will forget about trees,' she announced, 'or at least that is what I am aiming for!'

She selected a scarlet dress with transparent sleeves, the skirt reaching her ankles. With her black hair piled on top of her head, long dangling ear-rings, and a barbaric gold neckless round her slender throat, she looked more than striking. She made up her eyes with long lines from the outer corners to give them an extra slant, and on her feet she wore gilt high-heeled sandals. She came gliding into Damaris' room and struck an attitude.

'Will I do?'

'You look like Cleopatra,' Damaris suggested, thinking how well the slender scarlet figure looked against the dark panelling of the room.

'The serpent of old Nile?' She swayed sinuously. 'If only one of them looks like Antony!'

'Too much to expect,' Damaris smiled. She was wear-

45

ing her green silk and very little make-up. She felt insignificant beside Céleste's magnificence, her only ornament the silver bracelet with its lucky charms.

They came down to the salon where Monsieur and Madame de Valmond awaited them, Madame in faded lavender silk and Monsieur in a black velvet smoking jacket, long past its youth, yet both looked extremely distinguished. The dinner gong boomed and Monsieur frowned at the grandfather clock.

'Our guests are late.'

Hurried footsteps proclaimed that the guests were aware of their fault. A young man burst into the room.

'Christian won't be a moment,' he said in English. 'The landrover broke down on our way back and he got covered in grease. It takes a bit of getting off, don't you know,' then he giggled self-consciously as he saw Céleste. 'Oh, I say!'

'My daughter, Céleste,' Monsieur said repressively. 'This, my dear, is Monsieur Grieve.'

'How do,' said Donald Grieve, thrusting out a hand, while Damaris exchanged glances with her friend. Donald was tall and fair, but there his resemblance to Céleste's dream stopped short. He was fresh-faced and snub-nosed. He also wore glasses. Céleste touched his fingertips, while she smiled with satisfaction. She knew the young man was 'struck all of a heap'. That pleased her, though the conquest was hardly worth her metal. So much for Antony. To Damaris he spared barely a glance, he was plainly dazzled by her friend, and he shook her hand absently.

'We will not wait,' Monsieur de Valmond said, 'or the soup will be cold.' He held out his arm to his wife with old-fashioned formality. Donald, quick to imitate him, offered his to Céleste, and his proud air of proprietorship as he led her to the dining room made Damaris want to laugh as she brought up the rear. Céleste threw her a comical glance over her shoulder, and faintly shrugged. A poor thing, she seemed to say, but better than nothing. Damaris wondered what Christian was going to be like. They had finished the soup before he appeared, during which course Donald entertained them with an account of his day's work, which had been mainly clearing brushwood and marking 'whips' and 'wolves' for felling in the autumn. Upon Céleste demanding how on earth a tree could be a whip or a wolf, he explained the former meant slender growth without stability, and the latter misshapen trees that had outgrown their neighbours.

Céleste listened with praiseworthy attention, although Damaris knew she had about as much interest in forestry as a hungry lioness has in spring blossoms. What, she thought, a girl will do to get a man! They were waited upon by the same ancient Savoyard that she had seen in the garden, who seemed to combine several duties, assisted by a buxom country girl, and the newcomer slipped in obtrusively as the fish, local trout, was being served. He made a murmured apology to Madame, declaring that he did not require soup, and stood behind the vacant seat beside Damaris and opposite to Céleste, towards whom he threw a startled glance.

Monsieur de Valmond hastened to make the introductions. 'Monsieur Christian Trevor—Miss Damaris Treherne, my daughter Céleste.' Christian bowed to the houri across the table, upon whom his eyes were fixed, while he inclined his head to Damaris, before taking his seat.

'Monsieur Trevor, I am delighted to make your acquaintance,' Céleste cried vivaciously, 'whips' and 'wolves' forgotten.

'Reciprocated, but please call me Christian,' his voice was a little dry.

'But yes, and you must call me Céleste.'

Monsieur de Valmond raised his eyebrows, and his daughter turned to him. 'Do not look so surprised, Papa. Nowadays all the young people use the first name.' She had not been so informal with Donald. 'Christian,' she went on, 'that is not the usual name, *n'est-ce pas?* You will match with Damaris, her name is also uncommon.'

The merest flicker of blue eyes in her direction, blue eyes that were so familiar.

'It is,' he agreed, 'but I've met it before.'

Did he mean by that he had recognised her? He gave no other sign, but then he was plainly smitten by Céleste. Christian Trevor, the name she should have learned long ago if she had had her wits about her. Naturally he would not have an ordinary name like Tom, Dick or Harry. She flushed and paled, remembering all that she had told him about herself below the cliff at Ravenscrag. How much of that conversation did he remember? No wonder he had laughed at her naïveté, she had been a child, but now that she was much more sophisticated, she would be able to meet him on equal terms. He was as lean and bronzed as she remembered him, but tonight he was freshly shaved and neatly clad in a well-cut dark suit and a snowy shirt. She noticed that his cufflinks were gold and his whole appearance was expensive; only his hands betrayed that he was not the wealthy dilettante his sleek grooming suggested. They were calloused and toil-worn like Donald's from work with axe and sickle. So he was actually a forester, though he was in a different category altogether from his colleague.

She would have liked to engage him in conversation, show off her nearly acquired poise, but it seemed to have deserted her, she felt oddly shy of him, and Céleste gave her no opportunity. From across the table the French girl was doing her best to enchant. She fluttered her lashes, threw him sidelong glances, pursed her lips provocatively. Damaris had never seen her in action with an attractive man before, and she admired the performance. Monsieur, on whose right hand she sat, talked to her throughout most of the meal, so that she was more or less ignored by her other neighbour, who divided his attention between polite attentions to his hostess and parrying Céleste's badinage, with occasional heavy-handed interpolations from the neglected Donald.

After dessert, Madame de Valmond rose, signing to the girls to follow her. She adhered to the stately manners of a bygone age, when the ladies left the gentlemen to their wine.

'You will join us later for coffee,' she said graciously to the men.

Donald, who was nearest the door, sprang up to open it for her, a service that he had seen Christian perform upon other nights, and nearly fell over his feet in his eagerness to forestall his friend. Resolutely suppressing a desire to look back towards Christian, Damaris followed her hostess into the salon. Céleste subsided on to the sofa with a long sigh of satisfaction.

'Monsieur Christian,' he is *très gentil*,' she said. 'Maman, you will never make me believe that one is a forestry student.'

'That is how he describes himself,' her mother replied. 'I have not seen his papers, that is not necessary since we are not a hotel, but he spends all his time working in the woods, so it must be so. You are too romantic, *ma fille*. Is it that you think he is a prince in disguise?'

'He looks like one,' Céleste declared.

Madame de Valmond shrugged. 'There are no princes these days, or if there are, they are paupers, but that one is not a pauper, whatever else he is.'

'Ah, you intrigue me,' Céleste exclaimed. 'Me, I shall make it my concern to discover all there is to know about Monsieur Christian.'

Damaris too was curious about the fascinating forester, and with more reason than her friend. She had first met him falling down a cliff in Cornwall and had been too full of her own concerns to question why he was there or even to ask his name, but she felt reluctant to tell Céleste about that encounter, especially as she was not sure that Christian meant to admit to it. Yet there was no doubt whatever that he was the same person; she could not be mistaken, though it was an astonishing coincidence that he had turned up at Valmond. It certainly seemed that Mr. Christian Trevor got around!

Madame de Valmond meanwhile was expostulating anxiously with her daughter.

'He is our guest,' she was saying. 'You will do nothing that is not *comme il faut*?'

Céleste dimpled charmingly. 'Truly, Maman, you are old-fashioned,' she told her, 'but I promise I will not disgrace you in public—in private,' she looked mischievous, 'that is another matter.'

Coffee was brought in on a silver tray and with it came the men. Damaris watched with amusement Céleste's manoeuvres to ensure that Christian sat beside her on the sofa and not Donald. Having achieved her object, she leaned towards him making comments too low for the rest of the room to hear, but Christian seemed to find her remarks very amusing.

Damaris sat in an alcove, feeling a little forlorn, though she admitted to herself that she had no right to feel neglected because Christian was so taken with her friend. If he remembered her, he would also remember that she had told him she was engaged to her elusive Cousin Mark. She began to recall that conversation in detail. Since then she had come to realise that her marriage to Mark would be purely one of convenience. He could not, would not automatically love her because she had been bequeathed to him. That had been a childish illusion. For the first time she felt resentful of her grandfather's disposition of her fate. He should have left her free to choose her own mate, then she recollected that freedom meant that she would have to leave Ravenscrag and the place mattered more to her than any man. Granddad knew that and had ensured the only possible way to enable her to live there.

Donald, seeing Céleste was unapproachable, came across the room and dropped into an empty chair beside her.

'You look very serious, Miss Treherne,' he was beaming at her through his glasses. She smiled at him.

'I'm a little tired,' she told him. 'Everything here is strange, there's so much to absorb in a new place.'

'Ah, you're a guest too?' He lowered his voice. 'Bit overwhelming, isn't it? I sent some snaps of the place to my mum and she couldn't believe I was staying in such a palace. At home we live on an estate and our sitting room would about get into this corner.'

Damaris warmed towards him; he was a genuine sort of person.

'But perhaps you're used to this sort of set-up?' he enquired.

'No, though my home is a biggish house, it's very old and situated in Cornwall.'

'Really? It's a gorgeous part of the world. I've spent holidays there; but you can't depend on the weather. That's why people go abroad, the sunshine's more or less guaranteed.'

They talked about Cornwall, and soon she was describing Ravenscrag. During her recital, she became aware that Christian was looking at her, and across the width of the room their eyes met. He stared at her unsmiling, and it flashed across her mind that at last he had placed her. She smoothed the skirt of her green dress, and hoped he was thinking how much she had improved. Céleste sprang to her feet.

'Why do we do nothing but talk? I have the record player. Do you *messieurs* dance?'

'*Tiens*, Céleste, not tonight,' her mother objected. 'These gentlemen have to be up early to go to their employment, and it grows late. You must also be tired.'

'Me, I am never tired.' She ran across to a far corner

where the record player was housed, and Donald lumbered after her, anxious to assist. This incidentally was a Christmas present from Céleste's adoring parents.

'But I'm tired,' Damaris said. 'I think I will say goodnight.'

Madame rose from her chair. '*Alors*, I will take you to your room.'

It was Christian who opened the door for them. As she passed through a little tremor ran down Damaris' spine. She had forgotten how tall he was, how magnetic. He followed her into the hall and held out his hand.

'Goodnight, nereid.'

So he had remembered! His hand enfolded hers in a strong, warm clasp. She lifted her eyes to his, and met the quizzical glance that always disconcerted her; she remembered too that he had kissed her, the only kiss that she had ever experienced, and she blushed.

'I was wondering if you'd recognised me,' she said with more calmness than she felt.

He pressed the hand that he still held.

'Once seen, impossible to forget.'

Madame was waiting at the foot of the stairs; from the salon came the blare of the record player, and Céleste's voice calling Christian. He dropped her hand.

'Tomorrow we will talk,' he said. 'Sleep well.'

He went back into the salon and Damaris followed her hostess up the wide stairs pondering upon the strange twist of fate that had brought Christian Trevor back into her life.

Next morning Céleste expressed an unprecedented interest in forestry and asked her father to take her into the woods. The young men had breakfasted before the girls were up and were somewhere out upon a neighbouring estate. No one was deceived by Céleste's subterfuge. Her father said:

'*Ma fille*, I think you will be too distracting. Our

visitors are here to work for the good Monsieur Bonneville.'

'But I want to see what they are doing,' she insisted. 'Those "whips" and "wolves" sounded most fascinating.' Her brown eyes were full of mischief. 'I'm sure they'd welcome a break to say good-day!'

In the end she had her way and departed with her father in the old Renault. Damaris preferred to stay at home. She found she was reluctant to watch Céleste's conquest of Christian. It was absurd to be jealous, she told herself, and unworthy. Céleste had every right to subjugate Christian if she could. She herself was not free, even if she wanted to attract him, which she hastily assured herself she did not.

Madame introduced her to the kitchen, where it transpired she was responsible for most of the excellent cooking, assisted by two buxom maids, who had not yet discovered the opportunities offered by the cities. It was a huge stone-paved mausoleum with an electric cooker installed in one corner. The enormous hearth with its big fire—it could accommodate half a tree—gave a cheerful note, and there was no shortage of wood to burn at Valmond, but Damaris soon left its cavernous depths to wander out of doors. The neglected flower-beds were filled with daffodils, narcissus and irises growing in ragged profusion. She was wearing green trousers and a green tunic, and looked not unlike a flower herself, a bronze tulip with her crown of copper hair. She descended to the lower terrace down worn steps to find a lawn open to the view with cypress trees on either side, against the darkness of which some discoloured statues still stood. Tangled rose bushes behind the bulbs were in need of pruning, for beyond cutting the grass and pulling up the worst of the weeds, the place had been abandoned to the ravages of nature. She crossed the lawn and discovered yet another flight of steps with a rockery on either side, through which a tiny stream filtered. They descended to a sheltered walk, concealed from the Château by the rock wall behind it, and the stream dropped in a miniature cascade into an artificial pond where goldfish flashed among the lily pads.

'What a delightful place!' she said aloud.

'More civilised than Ravenscrag?'

She started violently. Christian Trevor was coming towards her along the paved walk.

'But ... didn't you go to the forest?' she stammered, taken off balance by his sudden appearance.

'It's not obligatory,' he told her. 'Don, poor devil, is bound to the treadmill, but I can please myself. Shall we sit?' He indicated one of the benches that were set at intervals in embrasures in the rocky wall. She seated herself demurely, smiling mischievously as she thought of Céleste enduring the bumpy woodland track in the old car in the hope of encountering the man who was beside her.

'What's the joke?'

'Nothing. But Monsieur de Valmond and Céleste have gone into the forest looking for you.'

Their eyes met.

'Well, they'll find Don,' he said. 'He'll be delighted to see them and show them what he's doing.'

Poor Céleste, Damaris thought, and hastily looked away. Something in the depths of the blue eyes undisguisedly studying her was disconcerting. He continued to stare at her, and aware of his scrutiny, she felt her colour rise.

'Are there fish in that pond?' she asked nervously.

'You know there are. How do you like school?'

'How do you know I'm at school?' she demanded.

'Monsieur and Madame have told us. The night before you arrived they talked of nothing but Madame Le Brun's unique establishment; how privileged you girls were to be accepted there. I must say she seems to have made a good job of you.'

'I wasn't always the little ragamuffin you met on the

54

beach,' she told him, 'even before Madame Le Brun got to work on me.'

'No? But you've learned elegance and poise. It'll be rather wasted at Ravenscrag, won't it? Or aren't you returning there?'

'Of course I'll be going back.'

He raised his brows. 'Do you have to?' His eyes narrowed. 'Does Cousin Mark insist?'

'Yes,' she said shortly. He was remembering too much. Actually her guardians had said nothing about the future after her year in Switzerland.

'You don't have to obey him,' her companion told her, 'or to marry him—I think that was the idea—if you don't want to. We no longer live in medieval times.'

She clenched her hands over her knees. 'I wouldn't dream of going against Granddad's wishes.'

'Still the grandfather complex?' The jeering note that she detested was in his voice. 'I should have thought you'd have grown out of that.' He leaned back on the seat and took out an expensive cigarette case. 'Smoke?'

'No, I never have.'

'Sensible girl. They say it's poison,' he said ruminatively, as he selected a gold-tipped Turkish, 'but we imbibe so many fumes these days, I don't feel tobacco in moderation is the most dangerous.'

The scent of tobacco mingled with that of the violets that grew in chinks in the rockery. Valmond was as yet undefiled by the poisons of civilisation. A fish surfaced with a plop and dived again, a flicker of orange and gold.

'You've met this elderly gentleman, your Cousin Mark?' he enquired silkily. 'Did he come up to expectations?'

'More or less,' she said, unwilling to confess that Mark had not bothered to meet her.

He gave her an enigmatic look. 'Was he like your

grandfather?'

'There was a strong family likeness,' she said coldly.

'How very satisfactory!' She glanced at him uneasily. Did he guess that she was romancing? But he could not know that she had never seen her cousin. She held out her arm. 'He gave me that for Christmas.' The bracelet at least was tangible evidence of Mark's interest. The charms jingled faintly. To her embarrassment, he took her wrist between his long brown fingers and with his other hand picked up and examined the charms one by one.

'Pretty, but unsuitable,' he commented. 'You should have had emeralds to match your eyes. He evidently considers you're still a child,' exactly what she had feared, 'but now you really look as if you've reached years of discretion, only I hope not too discreet.' Mockery gleamed in his eyes.

'My eyes aren't green,' she flashed, ignoring the remark about discretion. He dropped her wrist and took her by the chin, as once he had done before. Against her will, compelled by his magnetic gaze, she raised her lashes, and met his blue intense gaze.

'No, not green,' he murmured, 'or only in part. There's gold there as well—it would be difficult to find a gem to match them.'

He leaned nearer, and her heart beat quickly. In every nerve she was aware of him, but if he kissed her again, she must protest, and strongly. She was not free. But he did not; he drew back, dropping his hand.

'Your cousin was remiss to give you only that childish trinket, but then he can't know you've grown up.'

'There were some flowers as well,' she said defensively.

'With his love?'

She blushed scarlet. 'We haven't discussed love,' she said primly, then with a burst of defiance, 'I know you don't approve, but there's no other solution except marriage. We both want Ravenscrag.'

'Has he told you he wants Ravenscrag?' he asked.

She stared. 'Of course he does.'

Christian rose to his feet. 'It seems to me, my dear, you're taking your cousin's wishes very much for granted,' he said coolly. 'Anyway, I'm tired of the fellow. Would you like to come for a drive?'

'But I thought Donald had got the landrover?'

'So he has. I wouldn't dream of taking you out in that monstrosity. I've got my own car.'

She hesitated. It was a glorious morning, and she would love to see some of the countryside, but loyalty to Mark suggested it was not altogether wise to be alone with Christian.

As if he read her thoughts, he said impatiently, 'You're not in purdah, even if you do consider yourself engaged, and Mark is in Cornwall—presumably.'

Recalling her grievance against her cousin for his neglect, Damaris threw discretion to the winds.

'I'd love to come,' she said, and led the way back through the garden.

CHAPTER THREE

DAMARIS went upstairs to collect her handbag and sunglasses and touch up her make-up, while Christian went to tell Madame de Valmond that he proposed to take her guest for a run and obtain her approval; this was given together with an injunction to be back in time for lunch.

When Damaris returned, he had brought his car round to the front door, and she saw it was indeed far removed from the landrover, being long, sleek and expensive-looking. Everything belonging to Christian Trevor looked expensive. Yet he had come to this by no means five-star château in the company of a genuine forestry student, apparently to study trees. Damaris, like Céleste, scented a mystery and resolved to try to probe it.

The car descended the steep track to the village, nosed its way through a succession of minor roads and finally came out on to the main highway to Annecy, whence Christian announced he was taking her.

'Whatever made you come to an out-of-the-way place like Valmond?' she asked, for he had been chatting in a friendly relaxed manner and seemed approachable. 'I can't believe you're really interested in trees.'

'Can't you? Why not?'

'Well, you don't look like Donald.'

'Does one have to have a special type of physiognomy to learn about conifers?' There was laughter in his voice.

'You know what I mean, and there are bigger forests and better accommodation in other parts of Europe.'

'I happen to like this part, and working with Donald. He's an enthusiast. As for the accommodation, you're not being very polite to our hosts. I find them a charming couple, and the whole atmosphere of the Château belongs to a hundred years ago. That makes it so restful.'

'I think it's lovely,' Damaris said hastily, 'but then I haven't much to compare it with.'

'And that makes a difference?'

'Don't you think so?'

'You can believe me,' he said drily, 'when I tell you you'll have to go far to fare as well as we do at Valmond.'

'You, of course, having had a wide experience?'

'A very wide experience—and now let's talk about something else.'

Feeling a little snubbed, she dared not question further, and he began to tell her about the country they were traversing. Savoy was one of the smallest departments in France, and had originally been Italian. Most of it was mountains and the inhabitants were an independent, frugal people, who valued independence and their own way of life, and his discourse lasted until they reached their objective.

Annecy was a busy manufacturing town situated on the shores of a very beautiful little lake. The hotels were already filling up with tourists as the season was beginning. Christian suggested coffee, and they sat on the terrace of a café overlooking the lake. A party of climbers occupied a nearby table, noisy young people en route to the mountains, including several girls in ski-pants and woollies.

'Wouldn't you like to be going with them?' Christian asked, watching a pretty blonde, who, aware of his scrutiny, was preening herself.

'No. The only mountaineering I've done is scrambling down cliff paths, and I'd feel out of place with that lot.'

Some of the boys were unashamedly necking and she looked at them with distaste. Christian laughed at her expression.

'Do they teach prunes and prisms at your school?' he gibed. 'There's no harm in that lot, but they're not inhibited like some I know.'

'If you mean me, I've been taught good manners,' she said demurely.

'Ah, I was forgetting, I belong to the generation that hasn't got any,' she flushed, remembering how she had quoted her grandfather to him, 'but to returning to climbing pure and simple, it's fascinating. I do some most years.'

'Will you this year?'

'No. I shan't have time, I'm going to be rather busy later on.'

'With trees?'

'I've got other interests.'

'Such as?'

He merely smiled and took out his cigarette case; after lighting his cigarette, he laid it on the table, and she leaned forward to read the initials with which it was engraved. They were C.M.T.

'What's the M. for?' she asked idly.

'Why do you want to know, Miss Inquisitive?' he asked, pocketing the case.

She said with a spark of malice, 'It would be just too bad if it were Mark.'

'Why so? Your cousin hasn't got a monopoly, and the name is rather popular nowadays.'

'Is it? It always seems Cornish to me.'

'Because of the Tristram-Iseult legend? That's a favourite of yours, isn't it? I remember you called your dogs after that unhappy couple.' He hadn't forgotten a thing that she had told him. He leaned back in his seat, blowing smoke rings. 'I always thought King Mark was rather a sinister sort of character and, I imagine, elderly. Are you afraid your Mark may take a dim view of his Iseult amusing herself with Tristram in Savoy?'

'He wouldn't be so idiotic,' she began heatedly, 'and

there's nothing he could object to between you and me'—and blushed furiously, for her choice of words had been unfortunate.

'Not yet,' he said meaningly, 'but who knows what may happen? You may fall heavily for me. I've put a love philtre in your coffee.'

Involuntarily she glanced at her empty coffee cup, then laughed self-consciously. 'How absurd! How could you have done so, anyway? There aren't such things.' She strove to speak lightly, but was aware of a deeper under-current below his nonsense.

'Don't be too sure, and I'm a resourceful man,' he remarked airily.

She did not doubt it. She had been familiar with the Round Table stories all her life. They had been the centre of her adolescent imaginings, being denied a more modern outlet. Although Helen Carew had conscientiously told her that the Morte d'Arthur was not history and Arthur had been a Roman Briton fighting the Saxons, while the ruins on Tintagel were Norman, the romances had been very real to her. She had been to Tintagel, and had been awed by the gaunt pile of rock, divided from the mainland by its precipitous gorge, and had climbed the ladder of steps on to its windy height above the surging sea. She had identified herself with the lonely Iseult, married to Mark of Cornwall, yearning for the knight who had brought her from Ireland, and on the voyage drunk with her the potion that had caused them to fall in love. Christian's approach was subtle, for by linking her with the legend, he was suggesting a parallel, but though her King Mark waited for her in Cornwall, he had not been sent to bring her to him.

'Anyway, you're not in the least my idea of Tristram,' she said untruthfully, for he would have made a good model for Tristram, Lancelot or any one of the more exotic of Arthur's knights.

'Really? You disappoint me. I thought I could look

the part, even if I don't play it.'

'Which of course you wouldn't dream of doing,' she said hastily, for there was a grain of truth in his teasing, he was altogether too attractive for her peace of mind. She went on almost at random to disguise her embarrassment, 'You ought to be Cornish, with the name Trevor. You know what they say? Tre, Pol and Pen are all suffixes of West Country names.'

'Now it's my turn to disappoint you,' he returned. 'Trevor, I believe, is Welsh.' He glanced at his watch. 'If we're to be in time for Madame's excellent lunch, we'd better be on our way.'

On the return journey he talked easily about sport and the scenery, and the uneasiness he had awoken within her died away. He had only been ribbing her about King Mark and there was no hidden meaning below his words, but neither had he really answered any of her questions; the only information that she had gained was that he climbed mountains. As a person, he remained an enigma.

Céleste had returned from her abortive expedition and over lunch she eyed Damaris reproachfully, while she said to Christian:

'I had no idea that you had the time off. I would have much preferred to go to Annecy than bump about in the forest. Do you have much free time?'

'I take it when it suits me,' he said indifferently, 'but I'm sure your coming greatly gratified poor old Don and the memory will sweeten his sandwiches.'

Céleste preened herself. 'I think that he was pleased to see me.'

To make amends to her, Christian suggested that they should all four have an evening out, which drove away the last of her reproaches. Upon his return Donald agreed, as he understood Christian was standing treat. His own meagre budget did not run to evenings out. Monsieur and Madame were agreeable—they liked to see the young people enjoying themselves.

62

Céleste appeared for the expedition dressed in a black trouser suit trimmed with marabout and diamanté. She raised her brows as Damaris came downstairs in her green silk.

'Did you bring nothing else except that?' she whispered.

'Only one other evening dress. I wasn't expecting a whirl of gaiety,' Damaris told her.

'But, *ma chère*, you only had to ask. My wardrobe is at your disposal.'

Damaris thanked her warmly, but said she did not think she was the right type for Céleste's styles. She could not imagine herself in the exotic ensembles that she had glimpsed in Céleste vast wardrobe.

Christian made certain that they had their passports, as he was contemplating running into Geneva, a choice which disappointed Damaris, who was familiar with the town's shopping centre and would have preferred somewhere unknown. She was never sure how it happened, but she found herself beside Christian in the car, with Céleste and Donald firmly relegated to the back seat. He stopped en route in a small town, where a florist's stall still displayed its wares, and bought a bunch of sweet-smelling violets for each of the girls— purple for Céleste, but white for Damaris. As she fastened them into the front of her dress, she said:

'I suspect this is going to be a night to remember.'

'I mean it to be,' he told her.

Crossing the double frontier, the Geneva that then presented itself to her view was very different from the daytime city. Christian drove along a tree lined avenue by the waterfront, and all the myriad lights from the hotels and bridges were reflected in the lake, glittering jewels upon black velvet. From its eminence, the towers of Saint Pierre looked down upon them from the old part of the town, bathed in the glow of floodlights.

'It's a fairy city tonight!' Damaris exclaimed.

'The right setting for romance?' Christian suggested with a sidelong look.

They dined at one of the big, shining hotels. After a dry Martini by way of an aperitif, they ate lobster with prawn sauce, veal with cream sauce and fried potatoes, *petits pois*—a separate course, served with onions and butter, sweet and tender little peas, reared early in some glasshouse—and while the men chose cheese. Damaris and Céleste betrayed their youth by eating tipsy cake lashed with cream.

Christian ordered a bottle of golden sparkling wine, under the influence of which, Donald became almost gallant, paying both girls extravagant compliments. He even ventured to hold Céleste's hand under the table, which she, despairing of Christian, allowed him to do.

'Wonderful what a little stimulant will do,' Christian whispered to Damaris, 'even to a phlegmatic Englishman!'

'Aren't you English too?' she asked, surprised.

'With a Welsh name?'

'But the Welsh are British, aren't they?'

'But not English,' he returned. 'Actually I'm a bit of a mongrel.'

A mongrel, she thought derisively as he turned his well-shaped head to speak to Céleste. Every line of his lean, graceful body, his fine profile and long-fingered hands spoke of race. Perhaps when she knew him better he would tell her about his home and family. All she knew of him now was that he was travelled, unmarried—or so he had said when she first met him, though it did not follow that he was still unattached—and studying forestry—when it suited him. She remembered that Madame had said he was no pauper and he certainly was lavish with his money. The forestry, she surmised, was a whim, he could not be doing it from necessity, but of his real calling he never gave any hint. He turned back to meet her thoughtful eyes, and noticing her glass was empty, signed to the waiter to refill it.

'Oh, no more, please,' she protested.

'Go on, you've drunk nothing yet,' he told her, and leaning closer, whispered, 'this time it's the fatal draught!'

'Then I certainly won't drink it,' she said, pushing her glass away, and trying to speak lightly, unhappily aware that he might have spoken the truth. She was drinking a fatal draught, but it was not in the wine.

After dinner they went into the ballroom, which was all white and gold with crystal chandeliers, to dance. Christian dutifully divided his dances between the two girls, and each time she went to him after enduring Donald's clumsy performance, Damaris was aware of a thrill of joy. He moved with an effortless grace, and she had become expert at the Academy. Their steps fitted perfectly and he held her firmly but not too close. Amid the exotic figures of the other dancers, many of whom seemed to be executing their own version of the dances, he guided her with a smooth perfection that was almost professional. She told herself that it was because he danced so well that she was eager to be in his arms again, but knew there was more to it than that.

Once he said to her, 'Is the spell beginning to work yet?'

'Definitely,' she returned. 'This is a magic night, but it'll end at midnight, all the best spells do.'

For one evening surely she might be forgiven for forgetting Mark Treherne and surrendering to the charm of this most attractive man.

Actually it was well past midnight when they left for home. The big car ran fast and smooth along the edge of the lake, the moon had risen and threw a sparkling lane across the water, and silvered the distant mountain peaks, then their way turned away from the lake, climbing into the hills, checkered with black and white.

'Well, will you remember tonight?' Christian asked her.—

'All my life.' She laughed a little breathlessly. From the back of the car, Céleste murmured, *'C'était memorable. Monsieur est très gentil.'*

The Château appeared looking more than ever like a fairy-tale building; rising above the faint mist that lay in the valley, the moonlight illuminating its towers, it looked unsubstantial and ethereal. Behind it the woods rose, a black rampart to the sky. Only one light showed, that above the front door, everyone having gone to bed. Christian drew up in front of it, slid from his seat and came to open her door, while Donald handed Céleste out of the back.

'Donald, *mon ami*, you'd better hurry to bed,' Christian told him. 'You'll not have much sleep before you'll have to be up to go to work.'

Donald eyed him sleepily. 'From which I gather you don't intend to accompany me?'

'Not first thing, maybe later in the day. I'll leave the car here until morning.' While he locked it, Damaris stood in the drive beside him. Céleste glanced at them, shrugged her shoulders, and went past Donald into the house. He followed her, and the door closed behind them. Scent from the massed spring flowers below on the terraces drifted upwards, from the neglected rose bushes a nightingale began to sing.

'What a perfect night!' Damaris sighed. 'It seems a shame to go in.'

'Shall we go to see if the goldfish are enjoying it?' Christian suggested.

She hesitated. She knew she ought to go indoors, to linger alone with Christian was unwise, but she felt reluctant to leave the silver splendour of the night, to end this enchanted evening.

'Let's!' she cried recklessly, and lifting her long skirt,

ran lightly down the steps, across the lawn, and down the further steps, flitting as fleet of foot and insubstantial-looking as a nymph in her green drapery, and after her sped the dark shadow of Christian, a sylvan god pursuing her. She came to a halt by the pool, flushed and laughing. The moonlight sprinkled the water with diamonds, and a fish rose after some nocturnal insect, falling back with a plop, rippling the mosaic of black and silver. The scent of the narcissi filled the air with the incense of spring. She turned to Christian standing behind her.

'They're there, I saw one . . . Oh!'

For he had pulled her into his arms, holding her close. The perfume of tobacco and after-shave met her nostrils mingling with the crushed violets at her breast, and then all other sensation was blotted out as he kissed her, a kiss very different from the experimental one upon the cliff top. This one was masterful, possessive and completely devastating. Then, as suddenly as he had taken her, he released her. With her hand to her mouth, she again said inadequately, 'Oh!' The nightingale sang on, its flute-like notes quivering in the still air.

Damaris turned and went swiftly up the steps; reaching the little lawn, she began to run; she knew that he was following her, and sudden panic surged through her, and she increased her pace. She was running so much from her own feelings as from him. The catch of the massive front door baulked her, and for a moment of unreasoning terror, she thought they were locked out. His hand came down over hers on the handle.

'It's a little stiff, allow me to open it for you.' His voice was perfectly normal, and the wild beating of her heart began to subside.

The handle turned, and the door opened, but neither moved, though their hands had fallen apart, The flickering light from the lamp mingled with the moonlight behind them, she could not see him clearly;

he looked very big and menacing until she realised that he was laughing soundlessly.

'Little one, what's in a kiss?' There was a note of tenderness in his voice he had never used before. 'It's the proper way to say thank you for an outing. No need to run from me like a bat out of hell.'

'I see,' she said blankly.

'See what? Did you imagine I would try to seduce Mark Treherne's fiancée?'

The reminder struck her like the flick of a whip. She drew herself up and became immensely dignified.

'Of course not,' she said coldly, 'but I don't think Cousin Mark would like me to kiss you, even out of gratitude. Goodnight, Mr. Trevor, I gather my thanks have already been expressed.'

She swept past him and up the dim-lit staircase, aware of his now audible laughter following her.

When she reached her room, she found Céleste there, waiting for her.

'You've been a long time,' the French girl said suspiciously.

'I was only saying goodnight, and the door stuck...' Damaris turned to her mirror, aware that she was blushing and not wanting Céleste to see her confusion.

'How very convenient of the door!' Céleste commented drily. Her knowing eyes swept over the slight green figure with its coiled copper hair, now somewhat in disarray. 'I suppose he kissed you?'

'Well...' Damaris dragged her voice into a drawl, 'isn't that the correct way to say thank you for an evening's entertainment?'

Céleste laughed shortly, '*Alors*, he didn't give me much chance to say mine! *Eh bien*, *chérie*, congratulations, he's obviously deeply smitten and I withdraw from competition. Oh, but you have the good fortune,' she burst out. 'He is one in a million ... and now it occurs to me, he is something like the description you gave me of your dream man ... the one you met and did not expect to see again ... can it possibly be that Christian is he?'

Damaris nodded, and she went on, 'You had then an unfair advantage, a prior meeting. Did he know that he would meet you here?'

Damaris sat down on the dressing-table stool. 'Of course he didn't—it was pure chance, and you're jumping to conclusions. There's nothing whatever between him and me. Tomorrow perhaps it'll be your turn. I don't imagine he's over-burdened with fidelity.'

Céleste looked surprised. 'You mean if I could get him away from you, you would not be distressed?'

'Not in the least, in fact it would be best.'

Céleste was free, but she was not. Over her future loomed the shadow of Cousin Mark. She had an uneasy suspicion that Christian was deliberately trying to force her to break her engagement of which he had never approved.

'*Merci bien*,' Céleste said cheerfully. 'Since you have given me *carte blanche* I shall certainly try, though I do not think it will be of much avail.'

She rose off the bed where she had been sitting and came across to her friend, and leaned towards her, gazing into the girl's shadowed eyes searchingly. Damaris turned her head away. '*Mon ami*,' Céleste said gently, 'perhaps you make the mistake? I believe you have fallen for *ce brave jeune homme*.'

'No,' Damaris cried fiercely, 'I haven't, and I mustn't. She clutched Céleste's arm. 'Céleste, if you love me, never let me be alone with him again!'

'*Bon, chérie*, if you say so.' Céleste looked puzzled; was Christian after all a cad? She straightened herself. 'Do not fear, *petite*, I expect that I can—what you say —cope with him. Goodnight, *chérie*.'

After she had gone, Damaris sat for a long time on the stool, staring out of the window, where the curtains were drawn to admit the moonlight. To fall in love with Christian Trevor spelt sheer disaster. He had, she was sure, no serious intentions, and she must do her best to smother—and quickly—the unwelcome emotions he excited within her. Never again must she be so foolish as to allow herself to be alone with him. Céleste would help and the holiday was mercifully a short one. It was to be hoped that Christian would remember his neglected forestry. Once their association was over, there would be one more term at school, and then Ravenscrag and Sir Mark Treherne. Surely she could manage to discipline her unruly heart and keep out of his way during the brief interlude of this holiday? Outside in the garden, the nightingale was still singing. Resolutely she crossed to the window and drew the curtains shutting out the moonlight, the bird-song and the recollection of Christian's kiss. Cobwebs and moonshine, she thought, reality was the grey cliffs of her home where her heart truly lay.

Damaris' resolutions proved easy of accomplishment, for upon Donald reporting an infestation of pine shoot beetle, Christian became all forester and was off every morning to inspect the damage and discuss curative methods. The girls felt a little piqued— though Damaris was also relieved—to have to accept the humiliation of Myelophilus Piniperda's rivalry, but they had to realise that for the time being girls in Christian's mind were an inferior interest to the habits of beetles.

'He really is keen,' Donald told Damaris in response to a flippant remark of hers, 'forests seem to fascinate him and he wants to learn all he can.' They met every night at dinner, but Céleste had persuaded her mother to rearrange the seating and she took care not to allow her partner's attention to wander. Damaris concentrated hers upon Donald, who was always ready to be forthcoming about his work and prospects. He was hoping to get a job with the British Forestry Commission and his talk was all of planting, thinning and felling. Damaris during these lectures regretted that there were no forests at Ravenscrag. She could have given Cousin Mark a wealth of information. Christian threw her quizzical looks across the table from time to time to which she was careful not to respond. She did not find her self-imposed role of indifference easy. Often she longed to join in the gay flirtatious chatter on the other side of the table to which Monsieur de Valmond contributed his share, and sometimes tried to include her, but she implied politely that such triviality did not amuse her and she had only ears for Donald's monologues. Monsieur raised his brows and concluded that her '*yeux de diable*' belied her and she was that uninteresting phenomenon, an earnest Englishwoman intent upon improving her mind. A pity, he thought, for she had looks and charm, but she made no use of them. His own daughter was making full use of hers. The brown eyes sparkled, the white hands gesticulated, the pretty lips pouted and smiled. Christian seemed to enjoy the display put on for his benefit, watching the girl through narrowed blue eyes and answering her sallies with pungent wit.

After dinner, Céleste would pounce upon him as soon as he appeared for coffee in the salon and drag him off to put on her favourite records for her; the Château did not possess a television. Sometimes she would make him carry it into the spacious hall so that they could dance. Once during one of these sessions Christian came back for Damaris and requested that she would join them. She shook her head.

'Thank you, but not tonight, I'm a little tired,' she said coldly.

She watched him return to Céleste with wistful eyes. Her loyalty to Cousin Mark was costing her dear. Christian did not ask her again.

Some evenings later, he waylaid her on the wide staircase when she was retiring early to bed.

'Why the icy act? Have I offended you, or are you

71

afraid?'

He stood on the step above her barring her ascent, dark, magnetic, overwhelming. She looked up at him and saw in his eyes the quizzical gleam that always raised her ire.

'Of course I'm not afraid,' she said scornfully. 'Why on earth should I be afraid of you?' and was aware that her heart was hammering.

'For several reasons. To start with, you're not nearly so indifferent to me as you're pretending to be.'

This outrageous statement caused her cheeks to flame, and her eyes were all green, as she met his defiantly.

'You're absurd! Do you imagine every girl is crazy about you? You've got Céleste.'

'Perhaps I don't want Céleste,' he returned imperturbably. 'Don't you know that man's a hunter? He's intrigued by what's hard to get.'

'Really? But I'm not all that interested.' She tried to laugh, but the attempt was a failure. There was something hypnotic about his blue gaze. Her lips tingled in anticipation of his kiss, but he would not dare to do that here on the staircase where anyone might pass at any moment. Yet she was ashamedly aware that she wanted him to do so, and if he did, she would yield to him utterly. She stood motionless before him, fascinated as a bird is by a snake, but he made no move; fully aware of his power over her, he was savouring the final victory. At length with an immense effort, she dropped her eyes and said, 'Please, I'm on my way to bed. Goodnight, Mr. Trevor.'

He did not stir. 'I'm waiting,' he said meaningly.

Waiting for what? Desperately she was contemplating a return to the salon when to her relief Céleste came into the hall and called in her shrill voice:

'Chris ... Christian, aren't you coming? Where are you?'

He drew aside against the banisters to allow her to

pass him.

'Goodnight, Snow Queen—and mind you dream of me.'

She brushed past him, ran to her room, and threw herself upon the great four-poster bed in a sudden rush of tears. Was even Ravenscrag worth this self-immolation? If he had attracted her less, she would have dared to be her natural self, to join in his gay chatter with Céleste, but she knew that if she surrendered a single inch she would be overwhelmed—by what? Was this love that she felt for Christian? This inward turmoil when he looked at her this quivering longing for his touch? Familiar lines from *Tristram and Iseult* ran through her tired brain.

> *Let them drink it, let their hands*
> *Tremble and their cheeks be flame,*
> *As they feel the fatal bands*
> *Of a love they dare not name*
> *With a wild delicious pain*
> *Twine about their hearts again.*

She had needed no love philtre, no magic draught to cause her hands to tremble and her cheeks to flame, and she dared not name the emotion that had caused her disturbance. Nor must she ever acknowledge it, for she had no evidence that Christian was similarly affected. Challenged by her loyalty to Mark, he was amusing himself by trying to persuade her to betray it. He had been subtly clever to invoke the legend, knowing how it appealed to her, but, as she had told him, he was no Tristram, he was incapable of tragic passion, and if he had remembered the story accurately, he would know there had been another Iseult, she of Brittany, to whom the wounded knight turned for comfort and subsequently married. Céleste, to continue the parallel, could be well cast for Iseult of the White Hands. She remembered Sir Hugh's warning about the promiscuity and superficiality of the permissive society, and reflected that now she had met a member of it, all Christian wanted was a cheap flirtation. He had conquered Céleste and despised her accordingly, now he was stalking her in his dark subtle way, for had he not told her that man was a hunter? But if she surrendered to him, his interest would die, and she would have betrayed Mark and Ravenscrag for nothing. The holiday was nearly over, she had only to continue to keep him at arms' length for a little while longer and then she would never see him again. She rose from her bed, washed her face and prepared for bed, feeling very adult and very wise—and intensely miserable.

Two nights before the girls were due to return to Geneva, fire broke out in the forest behind the Château. Running out into the garden, Damaris saw the sky above the crest of trees that crowned the hill top was lit by a lurid glow, above which clouds of smoke obscured the first stars. Christian, Donald and Monsieur de Valmond hurriedly changed out of their evening clothes and went hurtling up the rutted track towards the scene of action in the landrover. Men from the hamlet below the Château followed, jabbering excitedly and carrying buckets and hoses. Madame de Valmond was busy at the telephone calling the police and fire services. Damaris went to discard her light dress for a jumper and skirt and returned to the garden.

The trees were black against the ominous glow and now and then a fountain of sparks shot up into the sky. A pungent scent of burning pine filled the air, and she could even hear the distant crackling of the fire. Madame de Valmond and Céleste came to join her. The older woman was wringing her hands.

'*Mon dieu*, it is a terrible thing, a forest fire!'

Céleste looked about her nervously. 'Are we in any danger here, Maman?'

'*Non*. The wind is the other way. The fire will not come down this side, unless the wind changes.'

Because of that possibility they did not go to bed that night.

Dawn came at length, the pure light stealing over the valleys and mountains between Valmond and Switzerland, but on the other side, the black pall still hung over the forest. With the daylight, Donald returned in the landrover with an exhausted Monsieur de Valmond. Both were filthy and blackened with smoke and grime. The forester came up to the house supporting the old man and both collapsed into the garden chairs set out before the front door.

'For the love of Mike—a drink,' Donald croaked.

Both girls flew to bring, beer, lemonade, anything that they could lay their hands upon. Madame was looking anxiously at her husband.

'You should not have gone, you are too old for such frolics, *mon ami*.'

'He did his stuff with the best of us,' Donald told them, after downing a pint of lemonade, 'but I guess he's had enough.'

'Where's Christian?' Damaris asked anxiously. 'Is he all right?'

'Wouldn't leave the battlefield,' Donald was beginning to revive. 'That man's a demon, tough as they make 'em, and he actually seems to enjoy fire-fighting.' He coughed. 'Drat this smoke, gets down your throat.'

'The fire is abating?' Madame asked.

'Not much.' Donald looked glum. 'It's been so unusually dry. They've got a fire engine up there, but there isn't much water, and the fire jumped the biggest firebreak—that's where we were working, beating it out as it came across, but it was gaining on the beaters when I left.' He passed his hand wearily across his blackened face. 'I must go back.'

'*Ah, non*,' Monsieur de Valmond exclaimed, 'you have done your share.'

'Every man is needed, and Chris asked for a flask of coffee.'

'I will go and prepare it,' Madame said, and hurried away.

'Monsieur Trevor is wise enough to know that coffee is a better reviver than a cool drink,' Monsieur de Valmond said. 'I only hope that he is alive to drink it.'

Damaris stared at him in horror. 'Is there danger?'

'*Naturellement*, but I did not mean to frighten you, Damaris, only the way that one was fighting—so reckless, so near the flames, I think he must have a charmed life.'

'Men like Christian always bear charmed lives,' Céleste said easily, and yawned. 'I think I shall go to bed, I cannot keep awake any longer. Do you come also, *chérie*?' Damaris shook her head and Céleste trailed away. Hith'erto she had not realised the fire-fighting might entail risks, and Monsieur de Valmond's words were not reassuring. She could not rest until she knew that Christian was safe. Madame de Valmond returned with a flask which she handed to Donald.

'And now, *mon vieux*, bed for you,' she said to her husband. He stumbled to his feet and she helped him into the house. Donald started towards the landrover, and Damaris ran after him.

'When will you be back?'

He shrugged weary shoulders. 'God knows—not until it's under control.'

Damaris could not face the hours of waiting; scruples and resolutions were submerged in a rising tide of anxiety. The sun was coming up in a blaze of glory, but the atmosphere was heavy and sulphurous; it oppressed her unbearably. Heavy smoke clouds were rolling down from the ridge, mingling with more natural cloud banking in the sky; she thought with apprehension of what might be happening upon the other side. It would be better to see for herself than to wait, her imagination working overtime. Donald swung himself into the driver's seat and let in the clutch; she clawed open the further door.

'I'm coming with you.' The vehicle shot forward with a jerk and she fell against the front seat.

'You mustn't,' he said flatly. 'It's no place for a woman up there.'

'Please. I promise I won't get in the way. I want to see what's going on.'

He was too tired to argue. 'Mind you stay in the landrover,' he told her.

They began to bump up the steep rutted ride. The trees on either side were dark and gloomy. Suddenly the road ahead was lit by a brilliant flash and thunder crashed overhead.

'If only it would rain!' Donald said hopefully.

'It usually does with thunder.'

'We need a deluge.'

It seemed he was going to get it, for by the time they reached the top of the ridge, the rain was streaming down, lit by intermittent flashes. The scene on the further side was one of desolation. The ground sloped downwards before rising to a greater height, and the downward slope was a blackened waste with the twisted trunks of trees still smoking, pointing gaunt fingers to the sky, and over all lay a pall of smoke and steam. The wind which had risen would lift a pile of ash, that glowed red, hissed and turned grey. Smoke obscured the bottom of the slope, but now and again a stronger gust would blow it away and Damaris could glimpse dark shapes flitting through the murk, or a sudden burst of flame, that sank and died under the onslaught of the storm.

'It looks like an inferno,' she said, appalled.

'It is an inferno,' Donald returned grimly. He drove a little way over the burnt ground and then stopped. 'It isn't safe to go any further, the ground's still hot.'

A tall figure came loping towards them carrying an axe with which he had been cutting firebreaks.

'Hi, Don, got that coffee? I'm parched—hell's got nothing on what it's like down there!'

Donald climbed out of the landrover and handed him the flask, while Damaris stared at Christian. He was stripped to the waist and his torso was grimy with soot and sweat, and striped with bleeding scratches. His hair was singed, his eyes bloodshot, but he held himself with a kind of reckless arrogance, and with the axe in his hand, he could well have been Thor the God of Thunder returned to earth.

'How's it going?' Donald asked.

Christian drained the last of the coffee.

'We're winning now,' he cried exultantly, 'with the help of the gods.' He waved his axe towards the streaming sky. 'Now there'll only be the mopping up to do.'

'I must go and find Pierre,' said Donald, referring to the head forester. 'Stay where you are, Damaris.'

'Damaris?' said Christian. Donald walked away and Christian came to the side of the landrover. The rain was streaming over his bare shoulders, washing off the filth and leaving them bronze. Damaris shrank back in her seat; there was something wild and primitive about his appearance and she was suddenly very much afraid.

'Come to view the battlefield?' he asked her.

'It's awful,' she said faintly.

'You're right, it is awful, but it's nothing now to what it was when it was blazing,' he laughed. 'Hot enough to melt even you, my little Snow Queen.'

Damaris wished heartily that she had not come. Her anxiety for him had been quite ridiculous. As Céleste had said, he was the type of person who would always come through on top. He was obviously excited and exhilarated and she hoped he would not suspect the emotion that had driven her to seek him. He threw his axe into the back of the landrover, remarking:

'That won't be needed again.' Then he reached up

and scooped her out of her seat and oblivious of the pouring rain, let her slide to her feet, keeping his arms about her.

'Did you come to look for me?' he asked her.

'Certainly not—I wanted to see——'

'Man fighting the elements?' he interrupted. 'I warn you, my sweet, I'm not civilised at this moment, and I'm ready to accept any challenge.'

A gust of wind tore past them, smoke blew into her eyes and nostrils, making her choke. About them the lightning flashed and the thunder rolled. His face was blurred, and the arms that gripped her were iron. His mouth when he found hers smelled of resin. The wild excitement that was pulsing through him communicated itself to her. Locked together amid the swirling elements, some primitive urge awoke in her. She raised her arms about his neck, yielded her body to his, and gave him back his kiss. Amid these surroundings of stark reality she could not maintain any pretence; she wanted him as much as he seemed to want her.

Other figures came tramping towards them through the murk. They fell apart, aware for the first time that they were both soaking wet. The mood of savage exultation died away.

Christian said, 'It's the first time I've ever kissed a girl in a thunderstorm. You'll always have that distinction, darling.'

Damaris turned from him towards the landrover while her heart sank. Was that all she was to him, the girl he had kissed in the rain? She heard Donald's voice.

'Are you both crazy? Damaris, you're soaked!' He dragged a couple of mackintoshes out of the landrover, while Christian declared, 'It's good to be crazy once in a while. Damaris won't forget this morning.'

'That I shan't,' she agreed. 'I've never seen anything like that fire.' She indicated the blackened landscape, while Donald draped the man's-sized raincoat over her shoulders. Christian's eyes met hers; his were full of mischief.

'There's more than one sort of fire,' he said meaningly, 'but alas, from your aloof expression, I'm afraid they're all out now.'

He lifted her up and unceremoniously dumped her on the front seat of the landrover. Pulling the other mackintosh over his shoulders, he turned to Donald and Pierre to arrange relays of men to watch that the fire did not break out again. Finally he climbed in beside her while Donald took the driver's seat. She sat sandwiched between them overwhelmed with weariness and half asleep. She was aware that Christian had put his arm around her to steady her, but even his clasp did not register. Her head with its tangle of wet hair dropped against his shoulder, while he discussed across it unconcernedly with Donald the fire and what could have caused it. Cascades of water from rain soaked branches fell upon the roof of the vehicle. Intermittent lightning still flickered among the trees, while the thunder reverberated from hill to hill.

'Are you nervous?' Donald asked her, after a particularly vivid flash.

'No. Should I be?'

'Good for Cornwall,' said Christian. The word gave her a jolt, for she did not want to be reminded of Cornwall or of Cousin Mark. She would like to go on for ever in this dream-like trance with her head on Christian's shoulder, the problems of the future shelved.

Donald wondered if she realised the lightning might at any moment strike one of the trees and bring it down upon them. Vaguely she was aware of the danger, but she did not care. If she were killed now, in Christian's arms, it would solve so much.

The storm had passed when they reached the Château, the rain settling into a steady downpour. Damaris was astonished to discover that it was only ten o'clock; the hours that had elapsed since she went with Donald had seemed like a lifetime. Looking like three scarecrows, they entered the hall where Madame de Valmond greeted them with upraised hands.

'*Mes pauvres .. ciel*, Damaris, is that you? I thought you were asleep in your room.'

'She came to rescue me,' Christian informed her gravely.

Madame looked puzzled. '*Tiens*, but all the English are mad!'

'Quite mad,' he agreed. 'Damaris, can you walk upstairs or shall I carry you?'

'I can manage,' she said hastily, sliding the coat from her shoulders.

'But you will eat ...' Madame began.

'Thank you, I only want to sleep.'

She hurried upstairs, fearful that Christian would seek to intercept her, but he seemed to have forgotten her. He was arguing with Donald which of them should have the bathroom first. Damaris threw off her wet clothes, sketchily washed away the worst of the grime and tumbling into bed, slept dreamlessly for eight hours. She was awakened by Céleste, dressed in an elaborate toilette, bursting into her room, demanding if she would get up for dinner.

'It is our last before we go back to school tomorrow,' she pointed out. She picked up one of Damaris' wet garments from the heap where she had discarded them. 'You should have given your things to Louise to dry.'

Damaris sat up, rubbing her eyes.

'I was too dead to do anything about them,' she explained.

'*Ma foi*, was it really necessary to go hurtling after him like that?' Céleste asked cattily.

Recalling all that happened, Damaris blushed. 'It was worth it,' she returned drily, 'and I'll come down to dinner.'

It would be her last sight of Christian and she could

not forgo it.

Dinner was late to accommodate the sleepers and they were all very quiet. Reaction had set in and they were very tired. Only Céleste had recovered her spirits, but she could win no response from Christian, who looked pale and weary. After coffee, Madame de Valmond suggested early bed and reminded the girls that they had still to pack. Céleste protested volubly. She had not experienced the ordeal the other had done and had been hoping for a gay evening. Christian, however, made it plain that he was in no mood for frivolity, and with difficulty concealed his yawns.

Looking at him shaved and groomed in his well-cut clothes, Damaris had difficulty in reconciling his civilised appearance with the wild-looking Viking of the early morning. She wondered if he were ashamed of that episode, though he did not look in the least sheepish when he took her hand, as she said goodbye—for as usual he would have gone to the forest before she was up—nor did he seem to have any regret for her departure. She had betrayed herself in his arms that morning, and now he knew she was won, he no longer wanted her.

'I hope you've enjoyed your holiday,' he said conventionally.

'Thank you, Mr. Trevor,' she said as coldly, but was unable to refrain from adding, 'I'll never forget the end of it.'

He did not, as she had hoped, respond to her lead. Smiling faintly, he remarked, 'It'll be something to tell your Cousin Mark.'

She hastily withdrew her hand. 'It will be, won't it?' she agreed, smiling sweetly. 'Especially your part in it.'

Next morning, waking early, she crept to her window for a last glimpse of him, despising herself for her weakness as she did so. The day was bright and clear as if there had been no storm on the yesterday. Her vigil was finally rewarded when he came past the tower, walking with Donald and talking animately, wearing his green forester's tunic and looking as fresh and alert as the morning. She carefully concealed herself in the curtain in case he looked up, but he did not do so. She was as far from his mind as if she had never been.

Later after breakfast the hired car—Céleste refused to travel to school in the ancient Renault—came to take them back to Geneva.

CHAPTER FOUR

THE summer term dragged out its tedious course. To Damaris, now nineteen, nearing twenty, her birthday was in September, school life seemed irksome, and since her womanhood was awakening, futile. It offered no alleviation whatever for the ache of her bruised heart. During the first weeks, being consumed by restlessness, she contrived to go into the town upon every pretext that she could devise—her hair needed setting, her eyes required testing, she even went to a chiropodist—her object, though she would not admit it even to herself, being to catch a glimpse of Christian bent upon some similar errand. Twice he had been precipitated into her life and against all reason, she could not wholly believe that he had gone out of it for ever. Then Céleste received news from home that he had left Valmond without finishing his course. Urgent private business, he had told Madame de Valmond, who bewailed his loss, but wasted no time in seeking to replace him.

'More antiquated females,' Céleste told Damaris disgustedly. 'Me, I shall not go home for the summer holidays. I have cousins in Paris, and perhaps something can be arranged. If it is, you will accompany me, yes?'

'Thank you, but I'll be going home,' Damaris told her, and trusted that she spoke the truth, for as yet she had been told nothing definite. She had received Céleste's news with a sense of desolation. In vain she tried to convince herself that it was a good thing, and it was her duty to erase all thought of Christian from her mind. The yearning for his presence seemed to increase rather than diminish. Resolutely she sought to concentrate upon her homecoming and in desperation she wrote to Mr. Preston, reminding him that her year abroad was nearly concluded and she was expecting to return to Ravenscrag. It was then that at long last that she told Céleste about her engagement, and her friend's reaction was typically French.

'Why did you think I would not understand?' she asked, 'the arrangement your *grandpère* made for you has much good sense. It is what we would do over here. Naturally milord wished you to be trained for your high position. You were when you came here,' she giggled, 'the little *gamine*, but now you can assume the air of a *grande dame* when necessary. Have no fear, your fiancé will be charmed when he meets you: I hope that you will invite me to visit you when you are established.'

'Of course I will,' Damaris promised, 'but it's the gap until I'm established that's worrying me.'

'Then do not let it do so. Milord will make the arrangements *comme il faut*,' Céleste assured her, but Damaris was not so confident. Cousin Mark did not appear to be making any arrangements at all.

Regarding Christian, she found Céleste's attitude slightly shocking. He, she declared, was not a man to marry. He would make a poor husband, but an excellent lover. Ascertaining that he knew Damaris' situation, she declared that he would be sure to reappear after her wedding.

'With an elderly husband, a woman expects to receive a young lover,' she announced. 'How else can she support life? But the affair must be managed with discretion. No hint to milord that you have an admirer, then one day he will come tumbling down the cliff again, and *voilà*, you will have it all, money, position and love.'

Damaris forbore to argue with her, knowing that she could not make her understand that such a triangular situation could not be tolerated. If she married Mark, she would owe him fidelity if she could not give him love. Nor did she think that Christian would ever come again to Cornwall. He had shown her plainly that he was indifferent towards her future.

Helen Carew wrote renewing her offer of a home. The shop, she said, had made a promising start. Her friend Mary Brooke was eager to include Damaris in her ménage, for they could do with further assistance. Mary had been widowed after only two years of marriage, and would be glad of help with her son David. The letter disquieted Damaris, as it suggested that she was not expected to return to Ravenscrag, but before she could write to request plainer speaking, she heard from Mr. Preston. He and his wife were coming to Switzerland for their summer holiday and he would be seeing her in Geneva.

She dressed carefully for the meeting, being anxious to impress him with her new sophistication. She wore a grey linen suit with a pale green blouse, a green hat, grey gloves and grey suede shoes.

'Very nice,' Céleste approved, 'but oh, so prim!'

'Mr. Preston will expect me to look ladylike,' Damaris said demurely. 'I could hardly go in trousers and coloured scarves, he'd throw a fit.'

'I fear me you are about to have an interview most dull,' Céleste commiserated.

As it turned out the interview was anything but that.

The Prestons were staying at an unpretentious hotel in a back street. Mr. Preston came out to meet her as she alighted from the taxi Madame Le Brun had hired to convey her. He looked a little older, a little greyer, but since he was holidaying in a continental town, he had assumed a slightly rakish air, overlaying his habitual dryness, which was a little comical. He shook her hand looking her up and down appraisingly.

'Well, Damaris, my dear, how charming you look. Come and meet my wife.'

Mr. Preston as a domestic character was almost as

unlikely as if a ledger had spawned, but not only had he a wife, he had also fathered a now grown-up family, and he was obviously gratified by the admiring glances Damaris received as he escorted her through to the lounge. His wife was a plump, pleasing little body, with no pretence of style, who greeted Damaris kindly. They drank coffee in the prim little lounge among the other guests, making small talk about the town and its environments, while Damaris wondered when her guardian was going to come to the point. At length he stood up and said:

'Now, Damaris, to business. The proprietor has promised that we shan't be disturbed. Excuse us, my dear.' He smiled at his wife, and ushered the girl into what was obviously the proprietor's office. Once they were seated, he stated without preamble:

'I'm instructed by Sir Mark Treherne to inform you that he is prepared to honour your grandfather's wishes and marry you, if you are agreeable.'

Damaris gave a sigh of relief. 'I thought it was all settled,' she told him. 'It was on that understanding that I agreed to go to school.'

'That was nearly a year ago,' he pointed out. 'You might have changed your mind.'

'It never occurred to me to do so. I thought I was bound.'

'That's the point, Damaris,' he said earnestly. 'Sir Mark is very anxious that you should *not* feel bound. He is quite ready to make a cash settlement if you would prefer to waive any claim to the estate, which I may tell you is generous, because most of the land is entailed upon the next male heir. It is only the Manor itself which is in question, and your claim to that depends upon this marriage.'

'It's the house I want,' she said shortly. 'It's my home.'

He looked at her kindly. 'Would it still seem so with a new master?'

Her lips quivered; the question was a shrewd one. Instantly she pressed them together and lifted her head proudly.

'But I shall be the mistress. I don't see any point in going into all this again; we all know what Granddad wished.'

'Sir Mark only wants to emphasise, and so do I, that you need not feel tied by Sir Hugh's wishes. They were a trifle—er—ill-considered, and I'm sure he would not have wanted you to fulfil them if they prove contrary to your happiness.'

She clasped her hands over her crossed knees and looked at him steadily.

'Do you think that it's impossible for me to find happiness as Cousin Mark's wife?'

Under the direct gaze of her candid eyes, his fell and he looked embarrassed. 'You've not yet met him,' he told her. 'He is considerably older than you are. I thought ... I wondered ... if you ... er ...'

'Had met someone else?' she helped him out. 'I was hardly likely to do that at school. Anyway, I'm quite sure I'll never meet anyone who could compensate for losing Ravenscrag.' She wondered as she made the statement—if Christian had loved her, could he have done so? But he had not loved her, and there would never be anyone else.

'You're taking an enormous risk,' Mr. Preston said with asperity.

'That's my look-out,' she reminded him. 'From all this I gather my cousin isn't very keen on marrying me.'

'My dear Damaris, what can you expect? As I said, he hasn't met you.'

Her lip curved scornfully. 'Whose fault is that? He could have done so any time during this past year if he'd been sufficiently interested. He could have come here now instead of sending you; I consider he's been downright rude.'

Mr. Preston made a deprecating gesture. 'He's very busy—renovations to the property, he doesn't want to unsettle you...'

'Rubbish!' she said energetically, her temper beginning to rise. The mention of renovations had not helped to soothe it. 'Let's get this straight. He wants Ravenscrag but not me, but I also want Ravenscrag, and I'm not going to let him turn me out of my own home. If he wants to live there he'll have to put up with me.'

Mr. Preston sighed. Damaris' reasoning hardly suggested a foundation for a happy marriage.

'Very well,' he conceded, 'I'll accept that, and now to practical details. You can't go to Ravenscrag while Sir Mark is in residence until you are married.'

'Why not? Mrs. Garth is there, isn't she? Won't she be sufficient chaperone?'

'No, and Sir Mark wouldn't hear of it. He has his position in the county to consider—and yours.'

'Really? Stuffy, isn't he? I'm surprised he considers me at all. But what's to become of me in the interim? I refuse to stay at school any longer.'

'Your old governess has kindly offered you a temporary home.'

'Indeed?' So that was the meaning behind Helen's letter. 'You've contacted her?'

'Naturally.'

'Without of course consulting me. And when does Cousin Mark intend to fulfil his share of the bargain?' Her eyes were all green and glinting dangerously.

'He suggests a year's engagement, while you get to know each other.'

She sprang to her feet, her eyes blazing. Had not she already been engaged to Mark for a year? If ever there were a laggard lover it was he!

'How very considerate of him!' she flashed. 'So for twelve months I'm to stay in exile until it suits his convenience to allow me to enter my home, during which time he may possibly find time to inspect me. I'm not a child any longer, Mr. Preston, to be ordered about. I'll go to Carrie because I've nowhere else to go, and *when* I do see Cousin Mark I'll have plenty to say to him, more than he'll want to hear. Meanwhile——' she remembered Céleste's invitation, 'I'll return when it suits me. I'm thinking of staying in Paris.'

'In Paris? On your own?' he looked horrified.

'With friends, and I shan't ask your permission, or Cousin Mark's, and you can tell him I'll die before I'll let him turn me out of my own home!'

Mr. Preston realised that further discussion was useless. His ward looked quite beautiful in her rage. She was as passionate and headstrong as all her race, and her husband would have his hands full if he tried to tame her. He shook his grey head mournfully—heaven alone knew what would be the outcome of this mad marriage which he was powerless to prevent. He suggested that the interview was terminated, and they should return to his wife.

The visit to Paris materialised, as Céleste's plans were wont to do. Damaris received a cordial invitation from the cousins, which she accepted with alacrity. It was her first independent action, for she knew that Mr. Preston did not approve, and she hoped it would be a slap for Cousin Mark, and show him that she was in no greater haste to make his acquaintance than he was to make hers.

The cousins comprised a family of four, the parents and a boy and girl, who lived in a pleasant suburb of the capital. When the young people discovered that Damaris was a stranger to Paris, they insisted upon showing her all the sights, even going as far afield as Versailles and Fontainebleau. Their strenuous days were concluded by sessions at various cafés, where students congregated and every subject under the sun was discussed. At last Damaris was associating with young people of both sexes belonging to her own age group, but although many of the boys made passes at her, she found them too youthful and callow to interest her. She warded off unwelcome attentions by declaring that she was affianced. During those hectic days the image of Christian receded, only occasionally a sight, or above all, a scent, particularly that of violets, recalled him to mind with the accompanying nostalgic ache. As for the complications surrounding her return to Cornwall, those for the time being she shelved.

Towards the middle of August, the respite came to an end. Céleste was summoned home, but her return to Valmond was mitigated by the hint of a possible suitor looming on the horizon whom her parents wished her to meet.

'Though I greatly fear he will not resemble our late lamented Christian,' she said wistfully, 'but no doubt he will have greater stability. *Eh bien, chérie,* when next we meet, it will be to dance at our respective weddings.'

They parted with professions of undying friendship, Céleste to Savoy and Damaris to England.

Damaris travelled by air to London and the Cornish express from Paddington. Helen had said she would meet her at the main line station, for most of the West Country branch lines had been closed. It would be a nice gesture if Cousin Mark brought her, Damaris thought, since he presumably had a car and Helen had not. But only Helen was on the platform as her train came in, and the sight of her ex-governess brought back a tide of poignant memories. Helen was completely unchanged. She was even wearing the same tweed suit that Damaris well remembered. Not so herself; in fact Helen did not recognise her until she ran up to her and kissed her.

'Carrie, don't you know me?'

'Damaris! What a metamorphosis! No, I didn't, you

look so grown up and smart.'

Damaris laughed self-consciously. 'Madame Le Brun had to do something to earn her fees,' she said wryly. She looked past Helen, seeking an elderly male figure, for she still identified Mark Treherne with her grandfather, but Miss Carew was alone. While they collected the girl's luggage, she told her that she had been lucky in obtaining a lift from a friend who had business in the town, and who would drive them home when she had completed it. While they waited for her, Helen suggested a cup of tea at the station buffet.

'She won't be long,' she said, 'it was fortunate she was coming in. Hired cars are expensive and the bus is impossible.'

'I'd be glad of a cup of tea,' Damaris agreed, thinking Cousin Mark might have offered to meet her if only out of consideration for Helen's pocket.

The buffet was almost deserted and having obtained their tea at the counter they sat at a corner table. Helen plunged into a voluble account of the progress of the shop, and it occurred to Damaris that she seemed to be deliberately avoiding more intimate topics. Though Mark had not come to meet her, she must, within the next day or two, encounter him, and she was longing to see her home again, but something in Helen's manner made her uneasy.

When Helen paused to drink her tea, she said perfunctorily, 'I'm glad everything is going so well, but what about Cousin Mark? Has he said when he's coming to see me?'

'He isn't,' Helen announced bluntly.

Damaris stared. 'He isn't? What do you mean? Why isn't he?'

Helen laughed shortly. 'I've been informed by Mr. Preston that you're to attend a formal coming-out party next month on your birthday, when the engagement is to be announced. It seems he wishes to receive you in state but is not anxious to meet you before he must.'

Helen spoke drily. She disliked the whole proceeding and heartily wished that she could persuade her ex-pupil to change her mind. Damaris flushed and paled.

'I've never heard of anything so insulting!' she gasped. 'Does he think I'm poison? I shall go to Ravenscrag and see him at once.'

'You wouldn't be welcome, and it wouldn't be very dignified,' Helen objected. 'I've heard the place is being thoroughly renovated, so no doubt he doesn't want you to see it until it's finished.'

'But I liked it as it was,' Damaris cried.

'Well, you must admit it was all getting very shabby and probably needed repairing,' Helen pointed out. 'Perhaps he's hoping to surprise you.'

'I don't want to be surprised, I'd have preferred to be consulted,' Damaris said angrily. 'It seems I'm to have no say about what he's doing, and he'll spoil it all...' She broke off, staring blankly at the serving counter, but not seeing it, her heart hot with resentment.

Helen stirred her tea thoughtfully, then said gently, 'The engagement's only a formality. If this man turns out to be quite unbearable, you can break it off.'

'And lose Ravenscrag?'

'My dear girl, the place is only stones and mortar, it's not worth a human sacrifice.'

'But it's my place,' Damaris said heatedly. 'The tenants have known me all my life, they're *my* people, not his. I belong there.'

'Ssh!' Helen said warningly, as a family came to the table next to theirs and proceeded to settle themselves, while giving them curious glances. Damaris calmed herself, and the newcomers soon became engrossed in discussing what they would eat. She said in a low voice to Helen:

'By the way, what's he like? I suppose you've seen him?'

'No,' Helen said shortly, 'and from all accounts he

93

appears to be a crusty old bachelor. Damaris, I wish you'd reconsider your decision.'

Damaris set her lips and said nothing, while Helen leaned forward and said urgently, 'You're still so young. Have you realised that you may meet a younger man? Someone you could love—when it's too late.'

The girl's lips quivered as a poignant memory of Christian stabbed her.

'A love they dare not name,' she whispered.

'What did you say?'

'Oh, nothing! I'm not romantic, Carrie, I don't think love's important and I'll never betray Ravenscrag for it.'

'Nor Sir Mark?'

'Nor Cousin Mark.'

The tiny seaport of Boscastle lay in a miniature gorge that wound tortuously towards the harbour and the sea. The main road to Tintagel descended into it and rose again still more steeply, rounding a hairpin bend, before pursuing its twisting way. A stream ran along the narrow valley floor beside the car park, on the further side of which, an inn, several shops and some houses clustered under the almost perpendicular rise of Penally Hill. Just before the highway crossed the bridge over the stream, a secondary road ascended sharply towards the main part of the town on the left, while on the right, a lane ran between the stream and the hill, bordered with cottages, souvenir shops and a witchcraft museum. Mary Brooke's gift shop was situated a little way up the secondary road. The visitor descended several steps into a tiny flagged forecourt filled with flowers in tubs. Above and behind the shop front were the somewhat limited living quarters.

'It's only a little place,' Helen said apologetically, when her friend's car had decanted them on to the road in front of it. 'I'm afraid you may feel a little cramped.'

'I shan't mind so long as I'm not intruding,' Damaris

said a little bitterly. Mark Treherne's attitude was very far from flattering and Helen had said nothing to soften it. She felt unwanted and alone. But not for long. Mary came running out to welcome her and kissed her warmly. She was a comely brunette, both shorter and plumper than Damaris, with beautiful brown eyes.

'Welcome, Damaris dear,' she cried, noticing the girl's forlorn air. 'I've heard so much about you that I feel I know you already.'

Behind her was her small son, a sturdy youngster of five years, with brown hair and eyes like his mother.

'David, come and say hello to Auntie Damaris,' Mary bade him.

'Oh, not Aunt, please,' Damaris objected, 'I'm not that old. Hi, David.'

The boy hung back, thumb to mouth. He was not going to allow himself to be hustled into intimacy with a stranger. Finally he removed his thumb and announced:

'Sol's got seven puppies.'

Damaris had already received this information, but in the stress of recent events had not considered it important. Now Sol's maternal effort promised to be the bridge between her and this small person.

'How exciting,' she said. 'Will you show them to me?'

'Oh, let the poor girl settle in first!' Mary laughed, hefting one of the newcomer's cases.

Frantic whines and scratchings betrayed that the dogs had identified Damaris's voice and were not going to be put off for any settlings in.

'Perhaps you'd better go and speak to them before they tear the place apart,' Helen suggested. 'Mary and I will take your luggage up.'

In the small back yard behind the house a rapturous reunion took place. Tris and Sol went crazy with delight, nearly knocking her down in their enthusiasm.

'The puppies are in here,' David informed her, opening a shed door, and the seven puppies, which were just old enough to be mobile, came tumbling out to add to the confusion.

'You *have* been busy, Sol,' Damaris laughed, trying to protect her stockings and skirt from being utterly ruined.

'I like feeding them,' David told her, 'but Mummy says you'll look after them now.' The brown eyes were wistful.

'You shall help me,' Damaris promised, 'and perhaps you'd like to keep one to be your very own.'

His eyes brightened and then clouded. 'I'll have to ask Mummy first.'

With some difficulty the puppies were returned to the shed, but their parents were allowed to follow Damaris into the house. They could not bear to be parted from her. Mary had prepared a meal, which included jam, Cornish cream and scones. 'Made specially for you,' she told Damaris. 'I don't suppose you had them in France.' Over this bounty, David, whose information about receiving a puppy had been met by a hopeful 'We'll see,' unbent.

'I likes you,' he told Damaris.

The girl's eyes misted. Cousin Mark had been remiss, but the warmth of welcome from her friends did much to atone for it.

Had Ravenscrag been nearer, Damaris might have fulfilled her threat of visiting her cousin, but it was somewhat inaccessible, for no bus service went near it, and it was too far to walk. Also her time was fully occupied, since the flow of late summer visitors continued unabated and she was often pressed into service in the shop, or requested to look after David, who did not start school until the following term. He and Damaris became fast friends and spent a lot of time playing with Sol's slowly decimating puppies, for they were old enough to sell, but Pluto, the smallest one, was David's own. Mary had rather jibbed at the prospect of keeping three large dogs, but Damaris had pointed out that when Tris and Sol returned to Ravenscrag there would be plenty of room for Pluto, and she fully intended her return should anticipate Mark's suggested year.

The days seemed to fly by and her engagement party approached with unexpected speed. She thought one of her school evening dresses would be quite good enough for the occasion. They had more style than anything she could obtain locally. She was far more excited at the prospect of seeing her home again than meeting her fiancé. She was still piqued by his neglect; he might at least have come to see her. She had been further mortified to receive a printed invitation card for the party, with the information typed on it that a car would be sent to fetch her, and she would be expected to stay the night. He could not even bestir himself to send her a personal note.

'I suppose there really is a Mark Treherne,' she said to Helen. 'I'm beginning to feel as if I were dealing with a disembodied spirit.'

'I'm afraid he's a very solid reality,' Helen returned tartly, for she too resented his neglect of Damaris, and thought it boded ill for the future.

One bright morning David came running in from the tiny front yard in a great state of excitement.

'Horses, Ris,' for this was what he had decided to call her, 'come and look!' He darted back again with Damaris in anxious pursuit. Pluto, who as a privileged member of the family had the run of the house now, was also excited by the three riders, who had paused outside the house, and he scrambled over the gate, which had hitherto baulked him. When Damaris reached the scene, he was running round the horses' legs barking. David uttered a squeal of anguish, unlatched the gate and ran after him, a forbidden procedure.

'Pluto, come back! Ris, Ris, he'll be hurt!'

The riders reined back their mounts, which were not appreciating Pluto's attentions. Damaris seized David and pushed him to the gate with the command, 'Stay there,' and went to capture the whelp. One of the horses, a chestnut mare, whinnied. Damaris, the puppy in her arms, stared at it.

'Sheba! she exclaimed. 'It's Sheba!'

Recognising her voice, the horse pulled towards her, to be wrenched violently back by the girl upon its back. This was too much for Damaris.

'Don't!' she cried sharply. 'She's got a tender mouth, she isn't used to rough treatment.'

The rider stared down at her in astonishment, while Damaris, the puppy squirming under one arm, reached up and stroked the glossy neck.

A man's voice with a slight foreign accent, said, 'Who is it, Rosita?'

'*Por Dios,*' the girl answered petulantly, 'how should I know? But perhaps she can tell us the way.'

Damaris eyes travelled up from the perfectly fitting jodhpurs and traditional yellow pullover to the lovely, sulky face above; dark eyes set in an oval face, coal black hair under a felt hat, full-lipped scarlet mouth.

'She knew your horse, and Sheba knew her,' said another voice. 'Is this by any chance Boscastle?'

'It is,' Damaris told her.

The second woman slid to the ground and passing her reins to the man, came towards her. 'Then are you Damaris Treherne?'

'Yes, I am, but how did you know my name?'

This woman was as dark as the girl on Sheba, but evidently much older, and her ample figure was not flattened by her riding clothes, though there was about her a ripe handsomeness that indicated that in more becoming garb she would be quite something to look

98

at. She held out both hands.

'I'm your cousin Elena, Mark's sister. I'm so pleased to meet you. How fortunate we lost our way.'

'Excuse me,' Damaris muttered, and hastily put the puppy behind the gate, then she turned to take the hands still extended towards her. Elena drew her nearer and kissed her on both cheeks.

'We're staying at Ravenscrag,' she explained, while Damaris recovered from this surprising greeting. She turned to the dark, foreign-looking man, who had also dismounted and stood watching her appraisingly, while he held the two horses, 'this is my husband, Pedro de Costa, and that is his sister Rosita. Our *estancia* in Argentina is next to the Trehernes'.'

Pedro bowed in a foreign manner, but Rosita ignored her, while Damaris racked her brains trying to place them. She remembered hearing vaguely that Cousin Mark had a married sister, but as she was domiciled in South America she had given her no thought. It came as a disagreeable surprise to discover that Mark was entertaining his family in her home from which she was excluded, and permitting Rosita to ride her horse. She had to fight a wave of burning resentment as she tried to respond civilly to Elena's greeting.

'I'd no idea you ever came to England,' she said, thinking that she had been made to look a fool. 'Cousin Mark might have let me know.'

Elena laughed. She had a gay, infectious laugh, and in spite of her annoyance, Damaris warmed towards her.

'I'm afraid we've stolen a march on him. I've been dying to meet you, but Mark said we must wait for your birthday dance next week, else we'd have come to call. I think he's planning some sort of dramatic introduction with us all in our glad rags, and now we've spoilt it all for him.'

'Rather childish,' Damaris said stiffly.

'Ah, but men can be surprisingly childish,' Elena

99

returned with warm tolerance, throwing an affectionate glance towards her husband, whose white-toothed smile lit up his swarthy face.

Rosita made an impatient movement and the chestnut danced. She was eyeing Damaris contemptuously and the girl became aware of her shabby skirt and blouse, which she had put on to help Mary unpack a consignment of new stock, and her untidy hair, which must contrast sharply with Miss de Costa's immaculate grooming. Rosita quieted her mount before saying in a deep, husky voice with a foreign intonation:

'So you're Marco's *novia*?'

'You're Spanish?' Damaris asked doubtfully.

Rosita de Costa smiled insolently, showing white, pointed teeth.

'No, Argentine, where we do know how to handle horses, though you doubted it.'

'I'm sorry. Seeing you on Sheba ... er ... surprised me.'

'Marco said she needed exercise,' Rosita explained, 'and since you were not available yourself ...' She shrugged expressive shoulders.

'I see,' Damaris said, again conscious of resentment. It was through no fault of hers that she had been unable to exercise Sheba, since her exile was due to Mark's unfriendliness. Since he had filled the house with his relations, she would have been adequately chaperoned and she had a better right to be there than the de Costas.

David leaned over the gate and pulled at her sleeve. 'Please, Ris,' he whispered, 'may I stroke that horse?'

'If Miss de Costa has no objection,' Damaris said punctiliously.

'Don't mind me,' that lady remarked, looking bored.

Damaris lifted the little boy, who gingerly stroked the mare's velvet nose. Elena smiled indulgently.

'You like children?'

'Yes,' Damaris said simply, while Rosita audibly

muttered, 'Tiresome brats.' Damaris lowered the child. 'He's my friend's little boy.'

Rosita's glance went to Mary's painted sign and window display.

'Your friend keeps a shop?' she asked disdainfully. 'I find that most odd.'

'Oh, things are different in England,' Elena put in quickly. 'Even the best families are in business now-adays.'

Her husband intervened, '*Cara*, we are far from home and must be on our way.' He bowed towards Damaris, 'it is a great pleasure to have met you, *señorita*.' He was a handsome, rather florid man, who had been eyeing her speculatively throughout the conversation. He helped Elena to remount, swung himself into his own saddle with the ease of an expert horseman, and saluted Damaris with his riding crop.

'*Au revoir*,' Elena called. 'I'll look forward to seeing you again at Ravenscrag!'

Rosita did not deign to say goodbye. The little cavalcade turned back the way it had come, but as they trotted away, Rosita's voice was carried back to Damaris on the breeze.

'Didn't they teach her how to dress at that ridiculously expensive school?'

'It was a lovely horse,' David said wistfully, as Damaris rejoined him.

'When I'm at Ravenscrag, you shall come and see Sheba often,' Damaris promised recklessly. Her face was flushed and her eyes sparkled irefully as she took him indoors.

'Who on earth were those people?' Helen asked, who with Mary had glimpsed the riders from the window.

'My fiancé's sister and his in-laws,' Damaris told her, 'of whose presence he hasn't seen fit to tell us.'

'That girl was remarkably easy on the eye,' Mary commented with genuine admiration, 'and she was beautifully turned out.'

'And darned rude,' Damaris said explosively. 'Carrie, somehow I must get into a town, even if I have to hire a car. I've got to have a new dress for this do next week.' She would show that insolent beauty that she knew how to dress!

She did hire a car, and taking Helen and David with her, they went to Plymouth for the day. Their road skirted Bodmin Moor, with Brown Willy and Rough Tor raising their brown heads on their right and Dartmoor, green and grey under racing clouds, looming ominously upon their left, but when they reached Plymouth the sun was shining brightly. Armed with a credit card and cheque book, Damaris raided the beautiful new shopping centre that had been erected in the centre of the town, which had been flattened by enemy action. She chose a white and silver gown, for she thought that Rosita would wear colour or black. That exotic Spanish beauty shrieked for brilliant shades or a sombre setting. The dress she finally chose was long, full and floating, masses of nylon over silk, with a sleeveless décolletée bodice trimmed with silver diamanté. She bought silver slippers and a silver fillet for her hair. That would have to be done locally, but the Tintagel or Boscastle hairdresser should be able to cope with it. Just why she felt such an urge to compete with the de Costa girl she could not quite explain, except that she had been needled by Rosita's contemptuous expression, her possession of Sheba and an uneasy suspicion that she might even aspire to Mark, who, she suddenly realised, might be considered a good catch. His dilatoriness in contacting herself might be explained by the presence of the Argentinian girl, which was an unwelcome thought, for she doubted if she had any legal claim to her home, if Mark repudiated her; it was only his sense of honour that bound him.

She completed her outfit with an evening velvet coat, with long full sleeves, trimmed with white fur. Her purchases made a big hole in her quarter's allowance, and for the first time she wondered exactly what she was worth. Mr. Preston's figures had conveyed very little to her.

On her birthday morning, she came down to discover an assortment of little parcels round her plate, presents from her friends. David was specially proud of his offering, another silver charm for her bracelet in the shape of a tiny horseshoe.

'You haven't got one like that, have you?' he asked anxiously. 'And you will like it best of all?'

'Yes, darling, I'll like it best, and it's the luckiest one of all.'

There was a letter and card from Céleste, who had written to offer her good wishes for her 'name day'. Her letter was a jumble of French and English, and thick with exclamation marks. She had met Armand Desportes, and she eulogised about his car, his flat in Paris and his promise to take her upon a trip to the States. 'All *très gentil*,' she commented. About the man himself she said very little, which was significant. She concluded by saying Damaris must come to her wedding, which would not be long delayed, and a hope that her friend's own affairs 'marched'. Damaris folded the letter with a little sigh. So much for girlish dreams of romantic heroes! Armand, she suspected, was neither young nor handsome, neither was Mark.

Mr. Preston sent formal greetings, Mark nothing at all, but he would no doubt produce some appropriate gift at the party, perhaps the long anticipated ring. She began to feel apprehensive about the evening. They were actually going to meet at long last, and how would he welcome her? What if he proved to be quite impossible? But, she thought, trying to reassure herself, he was after all a Treherne, and they must have something in common. His long sojourn in South America could not have entirely obliterated the Cornish in him. Elena, she reflected, had not shown much signs of it, but she had been friendly and forthcoming. Recalling her buxom figure, she hoped fervently that Max was not stout. A fat, elderly man would be disastrous. Sir Hugh had always been lean and distinguished-looking, even in old age.

Her appearance when she was dressed bolstered her confidence, for her mirror showed that she looked truly lovely. The long line of the dress gave her height and emphasised her slenderness. The burnished waves of her hair piled on the back of her head and bound with the silver fillet had a classical effect, while her arms and neck were pale apricot from the sun. She had carefully shaded her eyes so that they looked more green than grey, and lightly tinted her mouth. David, who had been permitted to see her in all her glory, exclaimed:

'Ooh, Ris, you look like the Snow Queen!'

Damaris winced. The last person she wanted to be reminded of at that moment was Christian Trevor. David, who had been having Hans Andersen's *Fairy Tales* read to him, went on, 'I don't wonder Kay went away with her if she looked like you do, but she wasn't loving like you, she had a heart of ice.'

Again Damaris winced. It was not in a spirit of loving-kindness that she was going to Ravenscrag but in a mood of defiance to claim her rights. At best she hoped she would find Cousin Mark was benign and kindly, though up to now he had shown no sign of either quality, but to be just, she had to admit that the inclusion of a young, and for all he knew, possibly flighty girl into his fixed bachelor life must present problems to him, and he must be a man of principle to have accepted her grandfather's behest. She resolved that she would do her best to show him that she was capable of maintaining the dignity of his position and hers, and to think regretfully of Christian Trevor was the height of disloyalty.

Unfortunately the car that came to fetch her was another reminder of all that she wanted to forget, for it was of the same make and colour as the one Christian had owned, and had driven her and her friend to Geneva upon that enchanted evening. The man who chauffeured it was unknown to her, a new addition to the staff, she supposed. Since she was to spend the night and return next morning, she had packed a case with a change of clothes and her night things. He took it from her ceremoniously to put in the boot, after opening the door of the rear seat for her. She wished he had been the old retainer who upon occasion drove her grandfather about, and she could have sat beside him in front and chattered of old days. Her solitary state in the back was a foretaste of her new position, but as soon as they turned off the main road into the winding lanes that led towards the Manor, the familiar sights drove all else from her mind. It was not yet dark and the September twilight revealed every well-loved landmark, recalling memories of her childhood and her grandfather.

The car slipped past the farms, where she had known every tenant; some she expected would be at her party, and the thought cheered her. Then the little church with its squat square tower came into view, with the cluster of whitewashed cottages around it, and finally the car turned into the drive, and the dearly loved façade of the house appeared. Every window was ablaze with light, streaming out between the undrawn curtains into the fading dusk. There were quantities of cars parked in the drive. Sir Mark must be entertaining all the neighbourhood that her grandfather had snubbed. She touched David's horseshoe on her bracelet, which she had tactfully put on since it was the only gift Mark had ever given her. She would need luck and all her newly acquired poise to sustain her through the ordeal before her.

The car slid to a halt before the front door of the Manor, which was set wide open, light spilling out on to the gravel. The chauffeur came round to open the door for her, saying, 'I'll see to your bag, ma'am,' and she walked forward towards the entrance. The hum of voices and the sound of soft music greeted her, as she paused in the doorway to stare at the unfamiliar aspect of the big, square hall, for it had been transformed. A chandelier hung from the high ceiling, a thing of glittering crystal that shed brightness into the once dim corners. A new parquet floor had been laid over the old worn flagstones. Banks of flowers, dahlias, roses, golden rod and michaelmas daisies, all the glorious colours of late summer were ranged round the walls, and up the sides of the wide staircase opposite to her, which ascended to a gallery running across the back of the hall, which was also decorated with pot plants. It looked alien and strange, and passionate rage surged through her. How dared he alter it all! The doors on either side of the hall were open, that leading to the dining room showed a glimpse of a table laden with food, gleaming glass, and cutlery, from what had been the drawing-room, the largest room in the house, the sound of music was issuing. Hired waiters crossed and re-crossed the hall, carrying trays of cocktails. Cousin Mark had organised this party with all the pomp and circumstance of a bygone age. Fresh from the informality of the student parties that she had attended in Paris, Damaris' anger was succeeded by an uncomfortable desire to giggle, and she hastened to compose her face. Mark belonged to the old school and had meant to do her honour with all this ceremony.

A bunch of new arrivals were between her and the staircase, being greeted by Elena, who was acting as hostess for Mark, on their way up to discard their wraps. As Damaris approached them, a group of men came out of the dining room going towards the ballroom coming between her and Elena. They stepped aside to let her pass, looking appreciatively at the slim figure in white and silver, with the light making a glory of her hair. Then one of them, a neighbour's son, whom she remembered vaguely as a gangling school-boy who in his holidays used to ride to hounds, recognised her.

'Miss Treherne!' he exclaimed, 'is it really you?'

'Yes, it's me,' she said ungrammatically, extending her hand, while she tried to remember his name. He shook it vigorously, and her eyes went past him to the other men, wondering which of them was Cousin Mark. The silver-haired distinguished-looking gentleman in evening dress might well be he. Only Mark would wear the outdated full regalia. He was smiling at her a little ironically, she thought. Yes, Mark might well be ironic, she took a half step towards him when she heard Elena's voice.

'Damaris, my dear, welcome home!'

Elena was a Junoesque figure in apricot brocade, her magnificent black hair piled high with a gold filigree rose amidst its coils. Behind her Damaris glimpsed Rosita, looking startlingly beautiful in a low-cut black dress with a gorgeous Spanish shawl draped around her shoulders. She stood between two men in dinner jackets, one of which was Pedro, but now Damaris saw the whole scene through a mist, for there was one who was not there, who would have derided all this display as a waste of time and money—Sir Hugh Treherne. Resolutely she blinked back her tears. She was about to carry out his wishes, ally herself with his heir, so both could keep their heritage. He should have no cause to reproach her for failing to fulfil her duty.

'How beautiful you look,' Elena murmured. 'Come and meet Mark.'

She slipped her arm round the girl's waist. Damaris looked round for the silver-haired man whom she had decided must be her cousin, but to her surprise he had disappeared. Instead Elena led her towards the taller of the two men beside Rosita. He was turned away from them, his head bent to whisper something to the Argentine, but as Elena called his name, he looked up and came towards Damaris holding out his hand.

'Welcome, Snow Queen, I see you've dressed for the part.'

Her startled gaze met the blue, amused eyes of Christian Trevor.

'You!' she gasped.

'Yes, Damaris, me—your Cousin Mark.'

CHAPTER FIVE

As Damaris climbed the stairs, her mind in a whirl, she was met in the gallery above by the housekeeper, Mrs. Garth, who had been on the lookout for her arrival. She at least was unchanged, a little greyer, a little stouter, but still the same motherly-looking woman she had known since babyhood.

'Oh, Miss Damaris, right glad I be to see you!' the good dame exclaimed. 'You're in your old room, and that Tom will have brought up your case by now. Come along, me dear.'

She led the way to the small bedroom at the back of the house, at sight of which a tide of memories surged over Damaris. Downstairs the house had looked unfamiliar in its gala dress, but here everything was as she remembered it. On the narrow bed she had slept every night of her childhood and girlhood, the shelf above it held her well thumbed books, including the *Morte d'Arthur*. On the walls were her much loved pictures, Landseer's stag in 'The Monarch of the Glen', Rosa Bonheur's 'Horse Fair', and Watts' 'Sir Galahad'. The curtained window would, she knew, look towards the sea.

'I thought you'd rather be in here,' Mrs. Garth went on, 'though Mrs. de Costa wanted to put you in the front. A right bossy madam she be, which I reckon's only natural, being the Master's sister, but them other two, they're real foreign, and Miss Rosita, she's a warm piece if ever I set eyes on one ...'

'I daresay,' Damaris interrupted, checking this spate of gossip. 'I'm glad to be back in my own room, and it'll only be for one night.'

Mrs. Garth looked dismayed. 'Oh, miss, the Master

said you'd be staying for a few days.'

'My friends are expecting me back tomorrow,' Damaris said firmly. Nothing had been said prior to tonight about a longer visit, and she did not want to prolong her stay. She needed to be alone to think and reorientate herself. Her predominant feeling at that moment was furious indignation. Christian or Mark (so the M. did stand for Mark!) had not played fair. When he had first met her he had been fully aware of the situation from the moment that she had told him her name. He had come snooping round Ravenscrag for a preview of his inheritance and his bride and had found her woefully lacking. He had spoken of the hayfields as being 'dirty' and doubtless he had thought her unkempt. So he had packed her off to school to be made presentable, and had come up to Valmond to inspect the result, without revealing his identity. He had deliberately led her on to talk of Mark, and had derided her loyalty. He had enjoyed deceiving her, it appealed to his impish sense of humour to play this dubious joke upon her. He must think that she had no heart and was determined to show her up as mercenary and calculating, but if he imagined that she was going to tamely surrender to him now, he would soon find he was mistaken; she had some pride left. That the purpose of this evening's entertainment was to seal her submission to Cousin Mark gave him all the trump cards, but she was not going to let him win hands down.

She slipped off her coat, and Mrs. Garth exclaimed at the beauty of her dress.

'My, Miss Damaris, but you've grown into a lovely young lady!'

Damaris smiled a trifle wryly. 'Sir Mark's masterpiece,' she suggested, a remark that went right over Mrs. Garth's head.

'If your grandfather could see you now, he'd be that proud of you.'

'Oh, please!' Damaris whispered, her lips trembling. She turned hastily to the mirror on the dresser to touch up her make-up.

'But Sir Mark'll take his place,' the woman went on. 'He'll be a comfort to you. Eh, but he's a fine man.'

'I'm glad you think so.' Damaris was tart. 'I expected him to be a lot older.'

'You don't want an old man, my lass. True, Sir Mark's no boy, but he's all the better for that. The place needs a man with know-how and guts to pull it round. It's been sore neglected.'

Damaris shivered as she began to realise the full implications of her situation. Hitherto Cousin Mark had been a vague, shadowy figure and she had conditioned herself to accept the thought of marriage to him with equanimity. But Christian Mark, virile and disturbing, was quite another proposition. She remembered how at Valmond he had pursued her with the lust of conquest, but he had never suggested that he loved her. He had let her go back to Geneva believing that she would never see him again. She had suffered while she had sought to quell the emotions that he had aroused in her, and he had not cared about, or even considered, her feelings. Knowing that she would return to him, he had been content to let the matter rest until tonight. Downstairs she had seen triumph in his eyes. The quarry was captured, to be used at his discretion after he had fooled her and forced her to deny her love.

Came a tap on the door, while a well remembered voice enquired, 'Can I come in?' Damaris' heart began to hammer.

Mrs. Garth opened the door. 'Yes, sir?' she queried. Mark brushed her aside and came to stand behind the white figure before the mirror.

'I've brought your birthday gift,' he said. 'I thought it would look well with your dress.'

She had forgotten it was her birthday. His eyes met hers in the mirror, his were full of laughter and he seemed to tower above her.

'I said it would be difficult to match your eyes, so I didn't try, but I think this will become you.'

He held up a glittering object, then moved nearer to clasp it round her throat. She quivered as his fingers touched the nape of her neck. The diamond necklace sparkled like a collar of fire.

'It's lovely,' she said breathlessly, 'but you shouldn't. It must be awfully valuable.'

'I'm not exactly a pauper even without Ravenscrag,' he told her, 'but actually that necklace is a family heirloom.' He reached round her to lay the case on the dressing-table, saying in her ear, 'Who but I should give you gems?'

She turned round to face him, gripping the table behind her with both hands. 'Are you trying to buy me?'

'Aren't you already bought?' He glanced towards Mrs. Garth. 'You can leave us now.'

The housekeeper hesitated, her sense of propriety shocked. Mark laughed.

'Miss Damaris is to be my wife,' he reminded her.

'Very well, sir.' She went out, but she left the door wide open. Mark looked appraisingly at Damaris, his eyes travelling from copper head to silver slippers and back again to her face.

'Madame Le Brun made a good job of you, my dear.'

'I'm glad you're satisfied,' she said sharply, her eyes glinting, 'but I'm not.'

He raised his eyebrows. 'No? Haven't you made sure of the home of which you thought so much? And aren't you pleased to discover that I'm not the old dotard you seemed to expect? I'm only just over thirty, Damaris, though I expect that seems a vast age to a teenager.'

'I'm not a teenager, I'm twenty today, as you know, and your age is immaterial. What I don't like is the masquerade. Was it necessary to deceive me?'

'The deception amounted to one syllable,' he said

lightly. 'My name is Christian Mark Treherne—Cornish, not Welsh. Was that so very reprehensible?'

'Yes,' she told him, 'because you deliberately misled me, and on the first occasion when we met, you didn't give me a name at all, Welsh or Cornish.' She smiled mischievously. 'I suppose what you found on the beach gave you quite a shock when I said who I was.'

'Your appearance was certainly unexpected,' he returned, 'but more so was your announcement that you were engaged to me.'

'But you knew the terms of the will. That's why you came, wasn't it?'

'To discover what I was letting myself in for? Partly, but the will didn't worry me; we could have found a way round it. Your insistence that you must marry your cousin did. However, before I parted from you I'd decided that you had possibilities and they were worth developing.'

Anger surged through her; how cold-bloodedly he had dealt with her! He had treated her as if she were a promising filly, which if properly trained, might one day make a racehorse.

'At Valmond,' he went on calmly, 'I saw how right I'd been, and if you hadn't been so blinded by that father-image you'd created, which I found very irritating, you might have guessed who I really was. Elena says the family likeness is quite unmistakable.'

'I never knew any of the family except Granddad,' she reminded him, but now, as she considered him, she saw there was a resemblance to the portraits of dark, hawk-faced men in the dining room downstairs, her ancestors and his, men whom she knew had been sailors and adventurers, masterful men, hot-tempered and arrogant. The discovery was not reassuring. She said firmly:

'All the same, it was mean. I'm not a detective, I couldn't demand to see your credentials.'

'Oh, come off it, Damaris,' he laughed. 'Was it so

despicable to want to see how the land lay before I committed myself?' (and to see if I were sufficiently improved, she thought angrily). 'You might have changed your mind, and in any case, wooing in disguise is in the best romantic tradition, half Shakespeare's plots are constructed round mistaken identities.'

'But you didn't woo me,' she flashed, 'you wooed Céleste.'

'And whose fault was that? I suppose I ought to commend your fidelity to Cousin Mark, it augurs well for our future, though I tell you here and now, you won't find me in the least paternal, but I didn't appreciate that silly French piece you foisted on to me. She . . .'

'Please,' she interrupted, 'Céleste is my friend, my best friend, and she'll be coming to my wedding, as I'm going to hers.'

'Oh, lord!' he ejaculated. 'I hope her husband comes too.'

'Always supposing there is a wedding,' Damaris suggested.

'There will be,' he said firmly. 'As you know, this do tonight is to celebrate our engagement, which I shall announce at supper with champagne and all the trimmings—and that reminds me, you must have this,' he produced an object from his pocket. 'I hope it fits, it's been cleaned. Mr. Preston told me it was your mother's and your grandmother's, the Treherne betrothal ring.'

As she made no movement to take it, he seized her left hand and pushed the gold ring with its single sapphire on to her third finger. He held her hand looking at her questioningly.

'What's the matter, Damaris? You've agreed to this contract, haven't you?'

Contract! Her eyes were on the blue fire of the stone in his pledge. That was how he regarded this marriage, as she had regarded it until now. As he had said, she had been bought with the price of her home. If he had spoken of love it would have made all the difference, but he had not. He did not even bother to feign an emotion that he did not feel, there was no need to do so. Right from the word go she had told him she was going to marry her Cousin Mark, and he did not have to exert himself to court a girl who was already his possession.

'Yes,' she said tonelessly, 'I agreed, but give me a little time to adjust to the situation. It was ... such a surprise...' She moved towards the door, and heard him say, 'A pleasant one, I hope?'

'That's what I'm trying to decide.' She turned on the threshold, her eyes challenging him. Oh, no, Christian Mark, she was thinking, I'm not going to fall into your arms like a ripe plum now you've chosen to unmask. You may have bought my consent, as you so chivalrously put it, but you haven't bought my love. That you'll have to earn.

'Shouldn't we join your guests?' she asked coldly.

He strode towards her. 'Don't I deserve a kiss?'

She eluded him, slipping into the passage. 'You do not,' she said over her shoulder, 'and I'm not sure I wouldn't have preferred an old dotard to a mountebank!'

She ran swiftly down the passage and he did not catch up with her until she had reached the bottom of the stairs, where Elena was waiting for them.

'Where have you been?' she exclaimed. 'We had to start the dancing without you.' She looked reproachfully at her brother.

'It was necessary to ring my fiancée,' he said casually, in the same tone that he might have used to say, 'ring the bull'. He drew Damaris' arm through his. 'We'll make our entry now.'

They entered the room together, where one swift glance showed Damaris that all the furniture had been moved, the floor polished, and, as she had surmised the

115

tenant farmers and squires of the neighbourhood were assembled there, complete with wives and grown-up children. Damaris slowly circled the room shaking hands with all those who were not dancing. Many remembered her and complimented her upon her appearance. She had the gratification of realising this surprised them, as much as her courtesy and poise. Many of them knew only too well that in their hatred of formality, their own offspring were casual to the point of rudeness. Then Mark claimed her for her first dance, a waltz.

'You've quite taken their breath away,' he told her.

'Yes, the ugly duckling's turned into a swan,' she returned lightly, 'thanks to Madame Le Brun.'

'You're hard on yourself. The nereid I met on the beach was easy on the eye.'

'A rough diamond then, that you decided wanted polishing.'

'Damaris, don't be so perverse. You know you needed further education.'

'Which you completed where Madame left off. What would you have done if I'd succumbed to your charming ways at Valmond? Repudiated me for a flirt?'

'I never forgot who you were and what was due to you.'

'Indeed? You didn't behave exactly like Sir Galahad on the day of the fire. Really, I'm surprised at you, Sir Mark Treherne! You quite forgot your knightly dignity that morning.'

'You weren't quite the little icicle you're pretending to be now,' he retorted, and she had the grace to blush. 'All right, Snow Queen, granted you're peeved by my little deception, but you'll have to surrender in the end, you know.'

She flushed and paled; he was so sure of himself and her, and she was not yet ready to yield to him, she needed reassurance, some sign of tenderness, of requited love, but the dark, arrogant man who guided

116

her so skilfully through the crowd of dancers looked about as capable of tenderness as a lump of their native granite.

As the dance ended, he said, 'I'm afraid I must do my duty by our neighbours, but I'm sure you won't lack for partners.'

Nor did she. There were many old acquaintances, or so they said—she did not remember any of them—who claimed the privilege of dancing with her and who in turn introduced their sons, who were eager to partner her. She caught glimpses of Mark battling valiantly with formidable-looking dowagers, but she noticed that he solaced himself by dancing with Rosita de Costa rather more often than courtesy demanded. The girl's sinuous body seemed to melt into his and her face wore an expression of near ecstasy when she was in his arms. Another of Mark's conquests, Damaris thought, and an uneasy doubt crept into her mind. Did Mark return the lovely Argentinian's passion for him? But she forgot it when Mark took her into supper, and during the toasts announced their engagement.

'It was what Sir Hugh wanted,' one old tenant declared. 'If only he were here to see this day. A right good sort was the old Master.'

Someone else said, 'The new one'll be as good.'

'I'll do my best,' Mark promised. 'I'll try to be a good landlord and a good neighbour. Already I love Ravenscrag. I feel I've come home.'

They've all accepted him, Damaris thought a little bitterly, and they've forgotten me. I'm merely his consort.

She danced once more with Mark, but he seemed aloof and preoccupied. The old magic that she had experienced at Geneva was no longer there. This to him was just another duty dance, as their marriage would be one of necessity. She felt that she had lost a potential lover and had not gained the paternal protector for whom she had hoped. To what manner of man had she pledged herself? He had usurped her place, stolen her heart and given in return a diamond necklace and a ring. She remembered that he was not all Treherne; he had from his mother the more passionate heritage of the South, alien blood that made him a little frightening and quite unpredictable. She became aware of a desperate longing for her grandfather, memories of whom lingered in every corner of the house. He had loved and shielded her in a manner Mark would never do.

The party did not break up until well into the small hours. Damaris stood beside Mark to take leave of their guests. The last to go was the old tenant who had wished that Sir Hugh were there to see that day. He was a white-haired, dignified old man, who remembered Sir Hugh in his prime, and Damaris when a child had often visited his farm. He lingered, talking about the old days, and when he finally took his leave, she found that Mark had disappeared. She went towards the drawing-room and hesitated upon the threshold. It appeared to be empty, until she caught sight of Rosita's shawl in a window embrasure. She was talking to someone, Damaris could not see whom, as the curtain masked her companion, and she was speaking in Spanish. Mark? Damaris hastily withdrew; neither would welcome her intrusion. Elena called to her from the dining room.

'Come and have a nightcap, dear, you must need it after all that.'

She went in and found Elena collapsed in an easy chair, while Pedro was helping himself to a whisky from the sideboard.

She looked round the once familiar room and now it was clear of guests, she saw that here too were changes. The old fireplace had been replaced by a handsome affair in imitation Tudor brickwork and the 'logs' it contained were fake ones in an electric fire. Velvet curtains replaced the well worn and well loved tapestry ones at the windows, and much of the furniture had been replaced. The long refectory table was the same, and the oak sideboard, but the dining chairs, though a faithful reproduction of period pieces, were new, so also the armchair in which Elena lolled; even the family portraits were not quite the same, for their gilt frames had been cleaned and retouched. Now that she could take in all the details of change, another wave of passionate resentment surged over Damaris. She felt she was a stranger in her own home.

Pedro came across to her, raising his tumbler.

'To you, *señorita. Por Dios,* I envy Marco!'

Mark, who was absorbed in a Spanish shawl in a corner of the drawing-room!

Elena asked if she would like a drink or something hot.

Swallowing her resentment, for the de Costas were not to blame, Damaris asked if she could have a glass of cold milk. Pedro gasped. 'Milk?' Then he smiled, 'Is that the secret of the roses and cream?'

'Perhaps,' Damaris smiled at the compliment, 'but the rose is wilting.'

'Tired?' Elena asked kindly; she seemed to genuinely want to be friendly.

'A little,' Damaris admitted. The evening had been an even greater ordeal than she had anticipated.

Milk was rung for and brought. Neither Rosita nor Mark appeared.

'It was all delightful,' Damaris said politely, putting down her empty glass. 'You must have worked very hard. Thank you so much.'

'I think it all went off very well,' Elena said with satisfaction. 'It was a mixed gathering, but Mark said we must invite everyone connected with the place. He was very much *le grand seigneur*, wasn't he? He enjoys being the Lord of the Manor, and you looked perfectly lovely.'

'Thank you.' Damaris was cool. Nobody seemed to

remember that she was by birth Lady of the Manor; her place had become entirely secondary. 'Now, if you'll excuse me, I'd like to go to bed.'

Elena rose to her feet. 'But of course, dear, I'll come and see you've got all you want.'

As they crossed the flower-decked hall, while Damaris wondered what further alterations they concealed, Mark and Rosita came out of the opposite room. He looked a little sheepish, but the girl's beautiful face wore a look of complacency.

'Damaris wants to go to bed,' Elena said, eyeing her brother reprovingly.

'Already?' He came towards Damaris, but she retreated to the stairs.

'It's very late, or rather early,' she said, miserably aware that there was a slight quiver in her voice. She went on more firmly, 'Goodnight, Rosita. Goodnight, Mark.' She did not look at him.

'But, Damaris . . .' he began.

She took no heed, but ran lightly up the stairs. At the top, she paused and looked back. Behind Elena's substantial figure toiling in her wake, she saw Mark was standing hands in pockets, a frown on his face, staring after her. She also saw Rosita sidle up to him and slip her hand through his arm.

When she was alone in the sanctuary of her own room, Damaris went to the window and threw it open wide. Air straight from the sea blew in fresh and cool and she could hear the distant wash of the waves. That would never change, but the Manor itself had entirely failed to rouse in her the passionate affection that she had once felt for it. The presence of the de Costas, the signs of Mark's possession had altered it beyond recognition.

She took off the diamond necklace and let it fall in a glittering heap on the dressing-table. Slowly she drew off her engagement ring and turned it between her fingers. The Treherne betrothal ring, but even that was strange. She had never seen it before; it must have been lodged at the bank. She supposed that she should have been in a state of rapture to discover that the man who had first touched her virginal heart was to be her destined husband, but there was a snake in her Eden, in the shape of a Spanish-looking girl who plainly held prior place in Mark's affections. Not surprising that he had been in no hurry to meet her while he had that to distract him. She had never expected love, that bewildering, overwhelming emotion that she had glimpsed at Valmond, to come into this arranged marriage, but she had not expected to discover a rival for her husband's allegiance. Now it seemed Mark was prepared to honour the contract, share Ravenscrag with her, but had no intention of giving her his heart. That he did not consider was part of the bargain, and she knew from the masquerade he had played with her that he could make of deceit a fine art. She was within her rights to object to his liaison with Rosita, but she could imagine the quizzical look that would come into his eyes as he pointed out that she had been prepared to accept an unknown cousin, regardless of former attachments to keep her heritage, and that she had obtained. True, Rosita would be going home, but Mark possessed property next to the de Costa estate. He would want to visit it from time to time—and Rosita. A most convenient arrangement—for him—she thought bitterly.

'Oh, Granddad,' she whispered, as if the old man could hear, 'you didn't know what you were doing. You've sold me to a man who loves another woman.'

She remembered then all Sir Hugh's diatribes against the rising generation. Mark belonged to the permissive society in which a man could conduct his love affairs with whom he willed. Honour, fidelity, pride were dead words, scoffed at by the new régime. Where women were concerned, they held no meaning for Mark. Suddenly she felt that she hated him, with a hatred so intense that though she did not realise it, it could only be the reverse of love. What was she going to do? Continue with this farce for the sake of Ravenscrag? She did not know. She dropped the ring beside the diamonds, the ring with which, as Mark had said, she had been bought, and crept wearily into bed.

Damaris was awakened by Mrs. Garth bringing in her breakfast tray. Being young, healthy and very tired she had slept well in spite of her troubled spirit.

'Good gracious,' she exclaimed, looking at her watch, 'is it so late?'

'No one's up yet,' Mrs. Garth said disapprovingly, 'except the Master, he's gone into Launceston on business. Them foreigners,' thus she described the de Costas, 'never do get up, nor go to bed neither. Sir Mark'll be back for lunch and he left word as you might like to ride with him this afternoon.'

'But I meant to go back to Boscastle this morning.'

'You can't do that, miss, Sir Mark's got the car,' the woman looked troubled. 'Oh, miss,' she burst out, 'you'd much better stay awhile and look after your own.'

'What do you mean?' Damaris asked sharply. Mrs. Garth looked confused.

'There, miss, reckon I didn't ought to say nothing, but we all wants you here, miss, and that foreign trollop isn't to be trusted.' With which cryptic utterance, she took her departure.

Damaris lay back on her pillows. So even the staff at the Manor had noticed the situation! She felt hurt and humiliated. She made an effort to eat some of the food before her, fearing to hurt Mrs. Garth's feelings if she did not, but the toast and egg were tasteless. Was even Ravenscrag worth the sacrifice of her pride? Could she possibly condone this triangular position? She remembered with a wry smile that Céleste had suggested a similar three-cornered affair with the positions reversed, but Céleste would never put up with a rival, or only if she herself had a lover. That was something Damaris would never contemplate, though it would serve Mark right if she did. She savoured the pleasure she would feel in telling him she loved another, but there was no other, and he was much too sharp to be deceived.

A knock on her door, and Elena came in wearing a négligée, her thick black hair in a plait. The Spanish element was much more marked in her than in her brother; while Mark took after the Trehernes, she had the thick creamy skin and dark, lustrous eyes of her mother's people.

'Did you sleep well, dear?'

'Yes, thank you.'

Elena sat down on the foot of the bed. 'It's a great pity we never met before,' she said. 'I should like to have known Great-uncle Hugh. By all accounts he seems to have been a fine man.'

'He was,' Damaris assured her. 'The bottom fell out of my world when he died.'

Elena put a sympathetic hand over hers. 'He more or less dropped us when my father married an Argentinian,' she said. 'He was terribly insular.' She sighed. 'That marriage wasn't a great success. Mother ran away in the end. Did you know?'

Damaris shook her head. 'All I knew about you was that I had cousins in Argentina. I ... I'm sorry. Were you very old when she ... went?'

'We'd reached our teens, so I suppose she thought we could manage without her, but it hit Mark hard. He was devoted to her, he felt she had deserted him.' She looked straight at Damaris. 'If you find Mark a little hard and cynical, that's why. He doesn't find it easy to love and trust again, but he needs love.'

'Don't we all?' Damaris returned. 'But Mark doesn't want love from me. All he's interested in is Ravenscrag.'

Elena looked surprised. 'What makes you think that?' and as Damaris did not reply, she went on, 'I've always wanted him to marry and settle down. He was so wild, always rushing round the world, but when we heard about your father's death, he knew he'd eventually inherit the title and he'd always been interested in Cornwall. Dad talked so much about it, I think he decided he'd wait to marry until he became an English baronet, and then he'd live in England.'

Damaris laughed shortly, 'Poor Mark, he didn't bargain for inheriting me. Did he know I existed?'

'Of course, but you being a girl couldn't succeed to the title. We all imagined...' She stopped and looked embarrassed.

'That Granddad would provide for me,' Damaris finished for her, 'but not in the way he did.'

'It was the obvious way,' Elena declared. 'though it was a pity you didn't meet Mark sooner. I believe Great-uncle had some idea of asking him to stay.'

'Yes, but he didn't know he was going to die so suddenly,' Damaris' lips quivered. 'He had ... spoken to me about it.'

'He left a letter to Mark consigning you to his care,' Elena informed her. 'Naturally Mark felt responsible for you and since you expected to marry him, and he needed a British wife to be mistress here, it seemed a very suitable arrangement and I don't see why it shouldn't work out. Lots of arranged marriages do. Mother's was the exception, not the rule.'

Damaris was thinking of something else. 'Your husband's place is next to Mark's, isn't it?' she asked. 'I suppose you see a lot of each other.'

Elena gave her a wary glance. 'Distances out there are much greater than here,' she told her, 'miles and miles of pampas.' She paused, then added significantly, 'We'll be going home soon and when we come back for your wedding, Rosita will be staying behind. I wouldn't have brought her this time, only she was wild to see England, and I thought the old affair was all over.'

'You mean there was something between Rosita and Mark?' Damaris asked sharply.

'Only a little flirtation, nothing serious—you know how it is with young people.'

'No, I don't,' Damaris said slowly. 'I wasn't brought up like that.'

Elena laughed a little uneasily, aware that she had blundered.

'You're still very young and romantic,' she said. 'One does not marry one's first love. Mine was a *gaucho* on the *estancia*, a most handsome creature, but Dad soon sent him packing. Pedro had money and a fine place. We've been very happy and I've never regretted my herdsman.'

'Yours was another arranged marriage?'

'But of course. In our class and country *estancia* mates with *estancia*. Believe me, it's the best way. I'm sure you and Mark will get on well.'

'Perhaps.' Damaris had her doubts about that. So Rosita had been considered ineligible because she was not English, and Mark wanted a Cornish mistress for Ravenscrag, but it was not a difficulty that could not be overcome if love were in the balance.

Elena patted her hand. 'You're riding with Mark this afternoon, aren't you? If you haven't brought riding clothes, I can lend you some jodhpurs.'

Damaris glanced wistfully towards the window. She would like to ride over the estate, revisit all her old haunts and feel Sheba between her knees again, even if it meant being escorted by Mark.

'Thank you,' she said.

Mark did not return until lunch had started, and it cost Damaris yet another pang to see him seated in her grandfather's place at table. Yet he looked very much a Treherne. On the wall behind him another Sir Mark

Treherne looked down, the painted eyes on the renovated canvas showing very blue beneath his black
brows, and the curve of his wig. The likeness was very
strong, yes, Damaris thought; she had been blind not
to notice it before.

It was not a comfortable meal. Rosita, who wanted
to accompany the riding party and had been told there
was no mount available, the horse Elena rode having
gone lame, sulked. Mark was silent and brooding,
throwing every now and again critical glances at
Damaris, and she, who had expected to return after
breakfast, was aware that the working skirt and sweater
she had packed to wear for her journey was hardly
becoming to the future mistress of Ravenscrag. Elena,
afraid that she had said too much to Damaris, was ill at
ease; only Pedro, who was cheerfully impervious to
atmosphere, seemed to enjoy his meal. When Damaris
asked if she could have the car to take her home that
evening, Mark raised his brows.

'You're in a hurry to get away,' he said. 'I thought
you'd spend a few days with us.'

'I didn't know that, and I've made no arrangements.'

'Are you then indispensable?' he asked sarcastically.
'I thought you were a free agent.'

She coloured at his tone. 'I've undertaken certain
duties,' she said evenly.

Rosita turned her insolent gaze upon her.

'Don't tell us that you have to serve in that ridiculous shop.' she exclaimed scornfully. 'That would be
most infra dig.'

'It isn't at all,' Damaris returned with heat, 'in fact
it's great fun, and I have to do something.' Her eyes
challenged Mark. 'Do you expect me to sit twiddling
my thumbs for the next twelve months?'

His blue eyes kindled in response, 'Perhaps we need
not wait so long if the time's going to be tedious.'

'It won't be in the least tedious,' she retorted, 'and I

should much prefer to stick to the original arrangement.'

Rosita laughed maliciously. 'Such a lot can happen in a year,' she said meaningly.

Damaris smiled at her sweetly. 'So it can,' she agreed.

Damaris put on the borrowed jodhpurs—actually they were Rosita's, Elena requisitioned them without scruple, as hers had proved too big for the much slimmer girl, and her own green sweater. She came down in some trepidation to find Mark waiting for her with Sheba and a big black gelding, the animal that Pedro had ridden when she had met the de Costas. Mark wore perfectly cut breeches and well polished boots, and looked both debonair and carefree. Sheba nickered when she recognised her mistress and Damaris gave her the apple which she had taken from the dessert on the sideboard for that purpose. Then Mark gave her a leg up and they trotted away. Conversation, to her relief, was difficult, as both horses were fresh. She noticed Mark had a superb seat on a horse, but that was only to be expected. Out in the open country she urged Sheba to a gallop and was away over the fields, taking walls and hedges with ease. Mark behind her cried, 'Race you!' and the black surged alongside. Sheba did her best, but she was no match for Mark's mount, which topped her by a hand and had a long raking stride. On top of the cliffs, Mark reined in and waited, watching her approach. She pulled up beside him, her hair blown into a tangle by the wind, her face flushed with the exercise. Beyond the cliffs stretched the craggy coastline, washed by a blue and emerald sea, reflecting the sky, its blue no bluer than Mark's eyes. She turned in her saddle to look back at Ravenscrag spread out below them, patches of green field, intersected by hedgerows, white farms with grey slate roofs, red cattle and white sheep, but conspicuously lacking in woodland.

'Your efforts in forestry were rather unnecessary,' she remarked.

'Since most of my life has been spent upon treeless grassland, trees fascinate me,' he returned. 'Besides, I needed an excuse to come to Valmond.'

She stiffened, for she had not forgiven his deception. 'And Donald? Where did you pick him up?'

'Oh, I advertised.' He moved his horse nearer to hers. 'What's the matter, Snow Queen? You've done nothing but try to brush me off ever since you came here.'

She was tempted to mention Rosita, but checked herself. He would think that she was jealous and she would not give him that satisfaction. On his tall horse he was above her and he bent down to look into her eyes, in which the gold flecks reflecting the sunlight, were then predominant.

'Where did you get those eyes?' he murmured. 'The Trehernes are all blue or black.'

'How should I know? A throwback, I suppose.'

'To Vivian, Merlin's witch?' he suggested.

'Oh, don't be absurd,' she said, aware that his spell was creeping over her. She would not yield to his magnetic charm, he had offended her too deeply. 'I'm going home.' She touched Sheba with her heel, but he forestalled her, catching hold of the mare's bridle.

'What's the hurry? Are you afraid to be alone with me? You're going to spend the rest of your life in my company, you know, so hadn't you better get used to me?'

She shivered slightly; suddenly the prospect scared her. The rest of her life sounded so irrevocable.

'I know quite enough of you to be going on with,' she said tartly. 'The rest will keep.'

'Prickly as well as cold!'

'Oh, what does it matter?' she cried, goaded out of caution. 'We've never pretended, have we, that we're marrying for anything except expediency.'

A gleam came into his eyes. 'Is that so?' he asked. 'Do

you know, Damaris, I would never have believed you could treat me like this.'

'You expected a malleable child,' she flashed at him, 'conditioned by that fine school you sent me to, but I'm not going to let you bully me!'

He released his hold of her bridle and drew back.

'I don't want to bully you,' he said quietly.

'Then don't pester me more than's necessary. There's no need whatever for you to pretend. I know you're not marrying me for love.'

His face sharpened, went bleak. 'Love? What's love?' he asked her.

Sheba began to fidget. 'Something you'll never understand!' Damaris flung at him. Too late she remembered that Elena had told her this man had been hurt by his mother's betrayal of his love, she should have spoken more gently, but that did not give him the right to hurt others, as he had hurt her. She let the restive mare have her head and as they headed towards home, Sheba broke into a gallop. She heard the thunder of the black's hoofs behind her and some atavistic terror of pursuit awoke within her. She urged Sheba to an even faster pace, and she did not slacken speed until she pulled up a blown horse in the stable yard. The chauffeur-cum-handyman, Tom, came to take her horse, as she slid from the saddle, shaking his head disapprovingly.

'My, miss, she's all of a lather.'

Mark rode in, his black brows drawn together in a heavy frown.

'Have you no more sense than to ride at that pace?' he snapped, looking at the mare's heaving flanks.

Damaris flamed scarlet at the well deserved rebuke. In her blind panic she had over-ridden Sheba.

'I haven't done her any harm?' she asked Tom anxiously.

'She'll be all right, miss. I'll rub her down and put a rug on her until she cools off.'

He led the mare away and Mark followed him leading his horse. Unwilling to encounter him again, Damaris ran into the house to bath and change.

Many, many times she had come in after just such a ride with her grandfather behind her and two wet and muddy dogs padding beside her, their feet making a pattern of wet rosettes on the worn stone of the floor. Then it had not mattered, but now there was a doormat upon which to wipe dirty feet and dogs paws would not be allowed to sully the shining expanse of gleaming parquet. The flowers had all been removed, and the walls now disclosed were freshly distempered above the half-panelling. There were signs of alien occupation too. A guitar (Rosita's?) on the oak settle, a Mexican blanket on the window seat, Mark's raincoat flung carelessly over a chair, his briefcase beside it. Of her own and her grandfather's occupancy no sign remained. Everything changes, everything passes; she had been foolish to imagine time could stand still. She walked slowly upstairs. It was no longer her beloved grandfather's presence that permeated Ravenscrag, but Mark's, he had set his seal everywhere, even the cliff path held memories of her first meeting with him.

She bathed in the newly painted bathroom, where the brilliantly coloured robe hanging on the door could only belong to Elena or Rosita. Back in her room she carefully folded and packed the white dress, thinking that only this, her own sanctum, had not been violated. She wondered what had been done to the front bedrooms, one of which, her grandfather's, she would have to share with Mark. Mark, who was an alien, a dark, forceful character who held her future in his strong, brown hands and could, probably would, break her heart. But it need not be so. She was only engaged and the bond could be broken. She had accepted it because she wanted to live at Ravenscrag, but the Manor was changed, it was his, not hers and he would do with it what he would, however much she protested.

He was master of both it and her and she did not want a master, she wanted a mate. The shadowy figure of the unknown cousin had never been quite real. Now she had met him he had become too much so, he overwhelmed her and as she realised the intimacy she must share with him, the hot blood rose in her cheeks; passion without the sanctity of love was somehow degrading. Would he pretend to himself that it was Rosita he held in his arms?

A maid came to summon her to tea. She went down reluctantly into the one-time drawing-room, where the furniture had been put back, but not as she remembered it. Here again fresh paint and polish were in evidence and over the mantelpiece was a new picture by a local artist; an oil painting of Land's End. Elena was dispensing tea from the silver tea pot, Rosita lounged in what had been Damaris' favourite chair, Pedro sprawled on the sofa. A cosy domestic group, but she did not belong to it, she felt dispossessed, a stranger. She saw with relief that Mark was not present, and Elena, misinterpreting her quick glance round, explained:

'Mark doesn't often take tea, it's an English habit he hasn't yet acquired, neither has my husband.'

Pedro was drinking something, but it was not tea.

'Since you say you must go, the car will be ready at six,' Elena went on, 'but you must come over and see us again before we go home.'

'Will Mark be alone here when you've gone?'

'Yes, but he'll be busy. He wants to redesign the garden. It's been a bit ... er ... neglected and he wants everything to be in order by the time you come to live here,' then noticing Damaris' expression, 'No doubt he'll consult you from time to time.'

Damaris was mute. She wanted to cry out that she did not want the garden to be redesigned. She had loved it as it was, wild, unkempt but beautiful.

Rosita said, 'The place was like a morgue, but Marco

131

has tried to make it habitable.' Her dark eyes flickered over Damaris with veiled contempt. 'He'll be paying us a long visit before the wedding.'

Elena said hastily, 'He'll be on his own *estancia*, he has to keep an eye on it from time to time.'

'Of course,' Damaris murmured mechanically. How often would Mark find it necessary to visit Argentina—and Rosita?

'But he'll be bringing you over when you're married,' Elena said brightly. 'We'll look forward to welcoming you.'

Rosita stood up. 'I'm going out,' she announced. 'I need some exercise, and since the horses all appear to be lame or over-ridden,' she gave Damaris a barbed glance; so Mark had told her about that—'I needs must walk. Goodbye, Miss Treherne,' she nodded towards Damaris, 'you'll be gone before I get back.'

As his sister left the room, Pedro frowned. 'What has—as you say—bitten her? She does not like to walk.'

'I'm sorry about Sheba,' Damaris said, 'but after all, she is my horse,' and she wondered if she could find accommodation for the animal at Boscastle.

'We know that,' Elena agreed. 'Had we been staying longer we'd have bought a horse for Rosita, but it hardly seemed worth while. I'm sorry if you didn't like her riding yours.'

'That's all right,' Damaris said quickly. 'Sheba had to have exercise and I wasn't here.' It was not the possession of the mare that was biting Rosita. Mark continued to absent himself, and at a quarter to six Damaris slipped out to the stable to discover if Sheba had recovered. She found Tom in the stableyard with his head in the bonnet of the car.

'There's nothing wrong with it?' she asked anxiously, when he came up for air. She did not want to have to spend another night at Ravenscrag.

'It's fine, miss, just a sooted plug. Your horse took no harm, as you can see. Be you ready to go now?'

'You're taking me?' She had expected Mark would drive her himself.

'Them's the Master's orders. I'll come up and get your case.'

'Right, I've only got to say goodbye.'

She did not know if she were relieved or offended by Mark's absence. Evidently he was annoyed with her for her conduct that afternoon. He was resentful as well as masterful. She took a short cut through the garden, her light footfalls making no sound on the grass. Rounding a clump of bushes, she stopped as if she had been shot. To the side of the lawn she was crossing, there was an opening in the tall yew hedge, disclosing a small secluded square in the centre of which was a sundial, a place where she had often played as a child. Through the gap she could see two figures entwined, and Rosita's voice, charged with emotion, was clearly audible carried to her by the breeze.

'Marco, it is impossible for you to marry that funny child. You know I love you—I, not she, am your true mate, we understand what passion is ... Oh, *amado mio*!' She changed into a flood of Spanish. Damaris could not follow Mark's reply, which was in the same tongue, but his low voice sounded equally passionate.

She hurried away, while a black tide of jealousy rose up and choked her. At Valmond, she too had thought she loved Mark, but he had never spoken to her with such emotion as she had heard in his reply to Rosita. She did not believe that she could ever wean him from the Argentinian girl, to him she would always be 'that funny child,' (how those three words rankled!) for whom he felt responsible, and to whom he would pay lip service, while his heart lay on the other side of the world, where Rosita would be waiting for him whenever he visited his foreign possessions. She would never be able to conquer her jealousy, and she was wise enough to know that it was a poison that would ruin her life if she were mad enough to link it with Mark's.

Jealousy lingers even when love is dead; only if she were completely indifferent could she accept the situation without heartbreak, and she was not indifferent. Mark's touch could still thrill her, though she despised and hated him. To yield to him would be to complete her humiliation. Even for Ravenscrag it was too high a price to pay, and the Manor had changed, the house would never again mean to her what it had done in Sir Hugh's lifetime. It only remained to extricate herself from a hopeless situation. Rosita was right. Marriage with Mark Treherne was quite impossible.

CHAPTER SIX

THERE was nobody in the hall when Damaris returned to the house. Relieved to be unaccosted, she crossed its shining surface and ran upstairs to her room. There was something that had to be done before she left the Manor, and she hoped that Tom had not yet collected her case. To her relief it was still there. Hastily she rummaged in its depths and took out the flat case that contained the diamond necklace. She put it on the dresser and slipped the heavy gold ring from her finger. A thought struck her—the articles were too valuable to leave about offering possible temptation to the domestic staff. The little maid who assisted Mrs. Garth was only a village girl, newly imported to be trained, and it was unfair to test her honesty. But she would not take the jewels with her, neither did she want to provoke a scene by returning them to Elena or Mark. She had had as much as she could take for one day. Arguments and recriminations could wait for another time when she had her friends round her to support her, or better still, she could ask Mr. Preston to inform Mark of her decision. She opened the drawer of the dressing-table and pushed the case and ring inside under a mass of oddments, relics of her girlhood, that now seemed so far away. Someone would some day have to sort that lot out, she thought dispassionately, and later, if she remembered, she would see that Mark was informed where she had hidden the jewels, and if he was anxious about the fate of the diamonds, it was no more than he deserved.

She refastened her case and went to the window for a last sight of the scene that she would never view again from that vantage point. Low clouds were coming in, from the sea, their shadows passing over the rising stretch of green uplands between her and the cliff tops.

'Forgive me, Granddad,' she said aloud, as if he stood beside her, 'but you were a proud man you wouldn't expect me to share my husband with another woman.'

Tom knocked on her door and asked if she were ready. She handed him her case and the evening coat, which was too bulky to get inside it. Her hand touched the soft fur. How little she had anticipated this ending when she had bought it, and now it would be completely wasted. She was unlikely to have occasion ever to wear it again.

'The car's at the door, ma'am, I'll meet you outside.'

So she was ma'am when he was the chauffeur, miss when he was the groom, she noticed with a flicker of amusement. He departed to go down the back stairs, while she debated whether to go in search of Mrs. Garth and decided against it. She was in a fever to be off and knew the housekeeper would keep her talking and make embarrassing remarks. She hurried down the main staircase, hoping Rosita would delay Mark long enough to enable her to escape without having to say goodbye to him. Her hopes were realised. Elena and Pedro were waiting for her in the hall, but there was no sign of Mark. She was able to take her leave of them composedly.

'But where is Mark?' Elena exclaimed. 'Pedro, go and find him.'

'Please don't,' Damaris said quickly. 'I . . . I saw him in the garden, we said goodbye then.' In a sense she had. 'He . . . he's busy.'

She hurried into the waiting car, aware that her hosts were looking at her with surprise. As it swept out of sight, Elena turned to her husband with raised brows.

'What can have happened? Why isn't he driving her? Do you think they've quarrelled?'

Pedro shrugged his shoulders. 'They are both high-spirited and passionate,' he remarked. 'There are bound to be tiffs, but the reconciliations will be most sweet.'

Elena gave him an exasperated glance; that Mark and Rosita were both missing was significant.

'It's a pity,' she told him, 'you can't keep that sister of yours in order, and a greater pity we didn't leave her behind.'

Again Pedro shrugged. 'She insisted upon coming, but when we return I shall affiance her to Manuel Ramos,' he said coolly. 'It is time she was married.'

'You should have done it before.' Elena's voice was unusually acid. 'I rather fancy you've left it too late.'

'Well, how did it go?' Helen asked, as Damaris came in after Tom had deposited her and her case on the doorstep. 'You look washed out.'

Damaris laughed, 'Not surprising, I didn't go to bed until four o'clock this morning.'

Helen's eyes were upon her ringless left hand.

'Where is it?' she demanded. 'Surely he's given you a ring at last.'

Damaris turned her head away.

'I left it behind. I ... I've changed my mind,' she said shortly. 'Isn't that a woman's privilege?' She dumped her case at the foot of the stairs. 'Carrie, I must go into Launceston tomorrow and see Mr. Preston. I want to know exactly how I'm fixed if I don't marry Cousin Mark.'

Helen's relief was mingled with dismay. Something drastic must have happened to cause Damaris to draw back at the last moment. She peered anxiously at the girl's pale face, noticed the resolute set of her chin, the shadowed eyes. The girl had been hurt.

'So you thought better of it,' she said with the dryness she always affected when disturbed. 'Wasn't Sir Mark what you expected?'

'Not in the least,' Damaris told her with forced

cheerfulness. 'He's a gay deceiver if ever there was one. I decided I could never be happy with him. Do you think we could keep a horse in the wash-house?'

David, who had come into the passage in time to hear this last remark, ran to her.

'Ooh, Ris,' he cried excitedly, 'do you mean the one I stroked? Are we going to have it here? Really? Truly?'

Damaris knelt down and put her arm about him, drawing him close to her. Here was much needed solace.

'Really and truly,' she said, 'and I'll teach you to ride, though Sheba's a bit big for you, perhaps a pony...'

'Hold on!' Helen laughed. 'Where are you going to accommodate your stable?'

'That depends on Mr. Preston. I may be able to rent a field and a shed somewhere.'

'Then you're going to live with us permanently?'

Damaris rose to her feet. 'If you'll have me.'

'Need you ask?' Helen was emphatic.

David whooped ecstatically.

Mary was equally pleased to hear of her decision, but beyond telling her that the engagement was broken, Damaris volunteered no details. Both women surrounded her with unobtrusive sympathy, surmising that in some way Mark had let her down. Helen hoped that in the fullness of time her ex-pupil would confide in her, but was too wise to question her. Damaris suggested she and David should accompany her to Launceston next morning, for it was a tedious journey to take alone, an invitation both accepted with alacrity. The town was near the Devonshire border, and was sprawled round an eminence that was crowned with the remains of a Norman castle. David was enthralled by a glimpse of the ruined keep, gaunt against the skyline.

'Ris, can we go inside?'

'Perhaps, if we've time.' She looked at Helen. 'Let's make a day of it. You ring Mary while I'm with Mr.

Preston, and see if she can manage without us. I'll meet you at the Castle Café afterwards for coffee.'

Preston, Poldark and Preston were housed in an old building in a narrow street with carved woodwork above its latticed windows—a suitable setting for the keepers of the archives, Damaris thought. She had rung up the previous evening for an appointment and was ushered straight away into Mr. Preston's office. The room with its walls lined with shelves of law books smelt of old leather and the dust of ages. Mr. Preston came out from behind his big desk to greet her. No aftermath of his holiday lingered, he looked as dry and dusty as his books. They exchanged commonplaces, while he ushered her into a round leather chair, then resuming his former place, he looked at her keenly through his glasses.

'Well, my dear, what has happened to bring you in such haste? You said the matter was urgent when you rang me at my home address last night.'

She told him, and his face furrowed with perplexity during the telling of her tale, from which she omitted Rosita's name.

'But, my dear girl,' he protested, when she had finished, 'I understood everything was settled. Sir Mark was here only yesterday to discuss settlement.'

'Sir Mark,' Damaris said, her eyes glinting, 'has deceived me.'

Mr. Preston cleared his throat nervously. 'Come, come, child, if you've had a lovers' quarrel...'

Damaris laughed a little bitterly. 'Believe me, there's no love lost between Sir Mark and me, in fact his affections,' she emphasised the last word, 'are engaged elsewhere. Under those circumstances, I think it would be immoral to marry him.'

Mr. Preston's face softened, and he said gently, 'You've been so sheltered, Damaris, you don't know anything about men. Sir Mark is mature, you can hardly expect that at his age he'd be without prior attachment, but of course they will cease when he marries you.'

'I can't be sure of that,' she said stiffly, recalling with pain Rosita's passionate voice and Mark's as passionate rejoinder. 'He's half Spanish, isn't he?'

'His mother was Latin-American, but you knew that. What difference does it make?'

'Only that Latins are proverbially unfaithful.'

Mr. Preston was at a loss. 'Sir Mark's your guardian,' he said sharply.

'I didn't need a guardian after I was eighteen,' she pointed out, 'so actually he's never had any legal hold over me.'

'He paid for your schooling.'

Damaris' eyes flashed. 'I was afraid he had, but Madame Le Brun was his idea, not mine. I'd much sooner not have gone there.'

'What exactly do you propose to do?' he asked anxiously.

'As I said, I'm prepared to give up all claim to Ravenscrag,' she said firmly. 'I think I've enough money to live on, or if I haven't, I can get a job.'

'I expect you'll find your income adequate if you're not extravagant,' he told her, 'and when you're twenty-one, you will have control of the capital.'

'So I could start a business?' she said, thinking of Mary.

'Yes, but think well before you realise it.' He looked at her sharply. 'Miss Carew been getting at you? She never approved of Sir Hugh's will.'

'She has not, but she's offered me a home, which I shall need.' Suddenly she looked very young and very forlorn. 'I'd like to have my things from the Manor, my books and pictures, and my horse.'

'That's perfectly reasonable,' he agreed, 'and I'm sure Sir Mark will be generous, but you've gone rather far to draw back now. I understand that your engagement had been announced and it will be reported in all the local papers.'

She clenched her hands, recalling her anticipations when she had gone to that party, and its unexpected dénoument.

'Yes, I suppose I have,' she admitted. 'We'll just have to let it ride, then later on, when all the excitement's died down, we can put an announcement, a very small one,' a flash of mischief showed in her eyes, 'saying the marriage will not take place—that's the correct wording, isn't it? It wasn't to be for a year, anyway.'

'Very well, Damaris,' Mr. Preston agreed. 'I'll send you full particulars of your income and expectations after I've spoken to Sir Mark; you're entitled to some compensation, I think, in lieu of your share of the estate.' He made some notes. 'Your personal effects and your horse will be requested.'

She gave a long sigh of relief. 'One other thing, I want you to settle everything for me. I ... I don't want to see Sir Mark.'

He raised his eyebrows. 'You mean this engagement is not being broken by mutual consent?'

She hesitated on the verge of a lie, then she said quietly, 'No, I want you to tell him what I've told you. I want your ... protection.'

Mr. Preston sighed. 'You can leave everything to me,' he said gently. 'Though no longer your guardian, I hope I shall always be your friend.'

'Thank you,' she said. 'At least Granddad made no mistake about you. I know I can always trust you.'

Outside in the street, she was aware of a lightening of her spirit. At last she was free of the shadow of Cousin Mark. For far too long she had allowed it to hang over her future. Of Ravenscrag she would not think, but it would be still there. When Mark had gone back to Argentina, as doubtless he would go from time to time, she would ride over when she knew he was absent and chat with Mrs. Garth, but she would not go down to the beach; he had spoilt that for her, for she could not see it again without recalling their first meeting. How hilariously funny it must have been to him when she had in her blind faith told him that she was engaged to Cousin Mark, who was himself. No, she could not revisit the scene of so much humiliation. His investment in her schooling would be a dead loss, she considered with satisfaction, for she would never become the figurehead for which he had had her trained. He must look elsewhere for a suitable Lady Treherne, and he would not look far. She sighed. Rosita as Mistress of Ravenscrag was something she did not enjoy contemplating.

'Anyway, thank goodness I had the sense to pull out in time,' she thought thankfully, 'but only just. Now I must do my best to put it all behind me.'

She hastened to join Helen and David at the café, and found them already seated at a table.

'Everything satisfactory?' Helen asked as she sat down. David, who was eyeing a plate of cakes on the table, said eagerly:

'I thought you was never coming and I'se so hungry. Now can I have one of those simply super cakes?'

Damaris laughed. 'Yes, we'll all have some of those super cakes and drown our sorrow in cream.'

Helen shot her a keen look. So she had a sorrow to drown, and she suspected it was not wholly the loss of Ravenscrag.

Mary had told Helen business was slack and they need not hurry back, so David saw the inside of his castle, which he found a little disappointing, but he enjoyed scrambling about the ruined walls. After lunch they wandered about the older part of the town looking into gift shops and comparing prices with Mary's charges. It was evening when they finally returned to Boscastle to be greeted by the news that Sir Mark Treherne had called during their absence. Mr. Preston must have telephoned him directly after Damaris had left his office, and he had wasted no time in coming to demand an explanation. She was thankful that she had missed him.

'And a pretty paddy he seemed to be in,' Mary told her. Mark had not wasted any of his charm upon her, he had been peremptory and intimidating, but Mary was not without spirit, and had revenged herself in her own way. With her brown eyes dancing with mischief, she went on, 'I told him I didn't know where you were and you'd gone out for the day with David. Of course he took it David was a boy-friend, which is what I meant to convey.'

'Well, it's quite true, he is my boy-friend,' Damaris declared, 'my very best one. Aren't you, poppet?'

David smiled doubtfully. 'I likes going out with you, but what's a poppet?'

'Something very nice,' Damaris assured him.

She was thinking with some dismay that she had been optimistic to imagine that Mark would take her decision lying down. He was too arrogant, too overbearing not to want to get his own way, or allow himself to be thwarted by a solicitor. But when his temper cooled, he would surely realise that she had taken the only possible way out, and would henceforth leave her in peace. A thought occurred to her.

'Was he alone?'

'No. He had that sultry-looking piece with him, the one who nearly rode David down.'

So he had had the effrontery to bring Rosita with him. Did he think she was quite blind to what was going on? Swift anger swamped her apprehension. If he did come again, she would tell him in no uncertain terms what she thought about that.

That night she was full of her plans. She would rent a shed and a field to house Sheba and the pony that she meant to buy for David. She would enjoy teaching him to ride. She was already paying for her keep, but if funds allowed she would like to help to expand the business and take a more active part in it.

'Helen may need your help,' Mary said with a blush. 'I might not be able to give so much time to the shop later on.'

Damaris looked at her questioningly and Helen said bluntly, 'Mary is thinking of marrying again.'

'It's for David's sake,' Mary explained quickly. 'I feel he needs a man, a father, though I hate the thought of putting anyone in Tim's place.' She had lost her husband in a car accident.

'You mustn't think of it like that,' Helen expostulated. 'Tim wouldn't want you to mourn him all your life. You're still practically a girl, Mary, and Dick Everett seems to be a nice, steady boy. David adores him, so there'll be no trouble there.'

Damaris remembered the fair-haired garage mechanic who always seemed to be making small purchases at the shop. So he was after Mary. She glanced curiously at the young widow. Mary was undeniably attractive and very feminine. It was not surprising that Dick admired her, but he had seemed to Damaris to be only a kid himself; with a shock she realised he must be several years older than she was; it was only by contrast with Mark that he seemed so juvenile, and Mary was probably his first love. She sighed. In spite of Elena's declaration to the contrary it would be refreshing to be a man's first love, not his—she wondered how many women Mark had loved, then pulled herself up sharply. His amours were no concern of hers and she was not even on the list.

Mary was saying, 'He's got good prospects; of course I'd still work in the shop, but we'd have our own home, with luck, and there'd be more room here for Damaris.'

The little house behind the shop did possess three so-called bedrooms, but the one Damaris occupied was little more than a cupboard. Mary must have progressed some way with Dick Everett to be thinking of accommodation.

'I don't suppose we'll have Damaris for ever,' Helen

pointed out.

'Oh, yes, you will,' Damaris said firmly. 'I don't intend to marry, ever. Carrie and I will be two spinsters together.'

Helen smiled but said nothing; she sincerely hoped that Damaris would eventually find the married happiness that she herself had missed.

'I'm only marrying for David's sake,' Mary insisted, still contending with her memories.

Damaris wondered if anyone ever married for love. They dropped the subject and began to study catalogues and discuss the new lines they might consider stocking for the next season.

'Business will be pretty dead through the winter,' Mary warned them, 'but we make up for it in the summer when the visitors arrive. It's amazing what they'll spend. The pottery and wood-carving goes well. How about some home-made sweets? Any good at cooking, Damaris?'

'My education was confined to acquiring the social graces,' Damaris said, glancing at Helen, 'how to walk, sit, converse and entertain, subjects which I fear were a waste of energy, but I daresay I'm capable of learning more useful arts.'

'You're capable of learning anything you want to,' Helen laughed, 'and I should know.'

'Yes—well, due to your excellent coaching I was placed quite high at Madame Le Brun's Academy. Socially I was a wet, but that wasn't your fault.'

So they talked and planned, while Damaris tried, and almost succeeded, in stilling the tiny ache in her heart. For Ravenscrag, she told herself, but it was not; it was for what might have been if Mark had loved her instead of Rosita de Costa.

Her gaiety did not deceive Helen, who glanced at her from time to time, noticing her flushed cheeks, the unnatural glitter in her strange eyes, that tonight were wholly green. After Damaris had retired, she came into

145

her room while the girl was preparing for bed. The roof sloped down on one side, and there was only room for the divan bed, a small dresser and a chair; most of Damaris' clothes had to be hung in the passage.

'You're a bit cramped in here,' Helen remarked, sitting down on the divan, while Damaris creamed her face. Mentally she was comparing their confined quarters to the spaciousness of the Manor.

'I'm not very large,' Damaris said brightly, 'and I've never had a big bedroom. My room at school had been a nun's cell. Appropriate, wasn't it?'

There was a brittleness in her voice that distressed the perceptive Helen. She looked searchingly at the mass of bright hair, but it entirely obscured the girl's face.

'Are you sure it's what you really want?' she asked. 'Damaris, you know I never approved of Sir Hugh's plans for you, but are you certain that you've made the right decision? You don't seem very happy.'

'I'm perfectly happy,' Damaris' voice came muffled through a tissue as she wiped her face.

'Mary said Sir Mark was very good-looking and she was sure he could be most attractive when he wanted to.'

'Too much for his own good,' Damaris said bitterly. 'Carrie, I ... I've met him before, twice—he pretended to be someone else. *He* wasn't prepared to buy a pig in a poke like I was, and when he finally decided that he could just bear to live with me, I overheard him making love to another girl, that sultry piece as Mary called her, and the affair's been going on for a long time.'

Helen traced the pattern on the quilted bedspread with one finger, apparently absorbed in this pastime. She had suspected all along that the trouble was emotional, and feared Damaris had acted too hastily. She said casually:

'But you're not indifferent to him?'

Damaris swung round in her chair to face her, her eyes glittering.

'I hate him!' she said fiercely.

'Don't be childish,' her ex-governess rebuked her. She had had her answer.

'I won't play second fiddle to that ... that dago!' Damaris cried violently.

'It mayn't be serious.'

Recalling that passionate exchange which she had witnessed, Damaris shivered.

'Too serious for me.'

Helen stood up and going to the girl, pushed the hair off her forehead, gazing tenderly into the flushed, angry face.

'You're not exactly plain, Damaris, in fact you've become a very attractive woman. Don't you care enough for him, and Ravenscrag, to fight for him?'

Damaris' long lashes veiled her eyes, and she sat motionless considering.

Once she had gone after Mark—or Christian as he was then—driving through storm and fire with a heart full of love and anxiety, and he had told her he would remember her only because she was the first girl he had kissed in a thunderstorm. He had parted from her then as conventionally as if she had been a mere acquaintance, and had left her to eat her heart out during that last interminable summer term at Geneva, torn with the conflict between her love and her loyalty to a mythical Cousin Mark. What had he been doing during that summer? He had not spent it all in England. He had been back in South America with Rosita. Believing Damaris won, he had shelved her until the time came to call her back to heel and take over Ravenscrag. Then with that easy charm of his, he had chained her with a diamond necklace and her mother's ring, and gone back to Rosita, making love to her upon the very day after their engagement. She raised eyes hard as emeralds to Helen's face.

'You forget,' she said quietly, 'I wasn't brought up in the permissive society. I was taught to respect truth, honesty and fidelity. I don't consider Mark Treherne is worth fighting for.'

Helen straightened herself.

'You should know best,' she said, and kissed her. 'Goodnight, darling.'

After she had gone, Damaris threw herself upon her bed in a storm of tears.

Mark rang up next morning. Damaris had answered the phone, and in response to her automatic, 'Brooke's Gift Shop,' he said. 'Is that you, Damaris?'

Recognising his voice, she hastily covered the mouthpiece and signalled desperately to Mary, who, thinking the call was for her, came to take it.

Damaris whispered, 'It's Mark. Tell him I'm not here, that I can't see him—anything,' and thrust the mouthpiece into Mary's hands. She retreated to the other end of the shop, aware that her legs were trembling and her heart beating fast. She certainly could not afford to meet Mark if the mere sound of his voice could produce such agitation within her.

A customer came in and diverted her attention from striving to hear what Mary was saying, but not very successfully. The woman she was serving thought she was half-witted, for she seemed abstracted, and she finished up by giving wrong change.

'I was as evasive as I could be,' Mary told her when they were alone, 'but he guessed you were here. You can't go on playing hide-and-seek, Damaris. Hadn't you better face him and have it out?'

'He's no right to pester me,' Damaris said angrily, 'and there's nothing to have out. Mr. Preston's told him all that's necessary.'

'He doesn't seem to think so. He suggested calling tomorrow, but I told him you'd be out. He didn't believe me, but you were going to take David to Bude, weren't you?'

'Yes,' Damaris said thankfully. It was David's last day before he started school and she had promised him a final outing. The child was looking forward to school with mingled apprehension and eagerness. He had the only child's passionate desire for the company of his own kind.

The next day was gloriously sunny, a return of summer, and they set off in high spirits. Arrived there, they spent a happy morning on the beach, choosing the spot where the river ran beside the sands, making pleasant paddling for the little boy without the alarms of the sea waves. The river ran in a loop round a sand-bank before reaching the sea, and sea-birds, ducks and a pair of swans, the latter with a brood of five grey cygnets, fished and bathed in its shallow waters. David was enchanted with them, as they all gathered round to claim a tribute of crumbs. Damaris had to be firm to prevent him from giving them all the picnic lunch that they had brought with them. While he splashed and shouted, she wondered why Mark was so anxious to see her. Now that she had relinquished all claim to Ravenscrag, surely he must be satisfied? It might possibly be that he wanted to arrange with her about the disposition of her belongings, and she began to feel foolish. If that were all, there was no reason for panic. She must steel herself for the inevitable meeting and hope that she could control her treacherous emotions. It was idiotic to allow herself to be so affected by the thought of seeing him; he was nothing to her, nothing at all, she insisted fiercely.

They ate their sandwiches, cake and fruit washed down with a bottle of pop and supplemented by ice cream, surrounded by the attendant birds. The sea-gulls were so tame they would snatch the bits from their fingers. Fortified by this refreshment, they crossed the river and walked along the breakwater that enclosed the bay, ending in a twisted pinnacle of rock, from whence they watched the surf-riders, whose performance David envied.

'When I'm a big man, can I do that?' he asked.

'Yes, and many other things,' Damaris assured him.

They walked beside the canal and admired the trawler berthed between its banks, then concluded with a cream tea at a café in the town. David returned home tired but happy, proudly displaying his trophies to his mother, a cellophane windmill and a beach ball.

'Which you could have bought here,' Mary pointed out.

'But these are special,' David declared. 'They came from Bude.'

Damaris looked questioningly at Mary, who shook her head.

'He didn't turn up,' she said in a low voice.

So Mark had given up, and Damaris felt curiously flat.

When David had gone to bed, Mary told them with slightly heightened colour that she was going out with Dick Everett for a drink. Helen and Damaris watched her departure in Dick's car. The young man looking attractive in a white knitted pullover, his fair, curly hair ruffled by the breeze, with Mary in a powder blue two-piece chattering gaily beside him. Helen said:

'She's kidding herself she's only doing it for David, but she's more than half in love with him.'

'They're well matched,' Damaris remarked, 'and I think they'll be happy.'

Next morning, David was dressed in his new shorts and blazer, and already looked the typical schoolboy. Mary sighed as she surveyed him.

'Quite a little man, aren't you, love?' she told him, adding to Damaris, as he turned to inspect himself in a mirror, 'The first day at school is a landmark in his life. I've lost my baby.'

'Perhaps there'll be another,' Damaris consoled her.

Mary nodded, blushing faintly. She had already considered that eventuality.

'I hope so, it would be good for David to have a brother or a sister.'

Damaris sighed too. She would have liked to have a brother or a sister, and a first day at infant school instead of the solitary ministrations of a governess. She had been defrauded of young companionship, but she loyally stifled the vague regret. Her grandfather had done his best for her according to his lights.

Dick came in when they were about to set out to suggest that as it was early closing and his afternoon off, he should meet Mary and David after school and take them both out to tea, a prospect that David hailed with enthusiasm. Then he had to hurry away to the garage, while Mary took her son's hand and they trudged up the hill escorted by Pluto on a lead. Damaris watched until they were out of sight, David continually turning to wave to her, then the entrance of a customer summoned her to her duties.

Eventually Mary returned alone, and put a protesting Pluto in the yard.

'He's very independent,' she said. 'As soon as he sighted some acquaintances among the small boys, he told me to go, but I'll be thinking about him all day. Roll on three-thirty!'

'It seems very quiet without him,' Damaris remarked, 'but he's got to learn to stand on his own feet,' and was washed in the spate of memories that phrase recalled. Well, she had learned to stand upon her own feet, though the proceeding had not be altogether painless, but she would never have the responsibility for guiding a child's first footsteps along life's path, since she had dedicated herself to spinsterhood. She stared unseeingly out of the window at the hill opposite, where the waving trees rose above the row of houses backing on to the Tintagel road. She might have borne a child to Mark, an heir for Ravenscrag, if

151

... resolutely she checked her thoughts and began to dust the shelves with feverish energy. Work was her panacea, and she had many plans. There was a rumour that the cottage next door was going to be put up for sale. When she obtained her capital next year, she might buy it and turn it into an ice cream parlour. There seemed to be an insatiable demand for that delicacy, especially if it could be described as made with Cornish or Devonshire cream. The bearded artist who had come to live across the way at Rose Cottage might do the decorations for her, and would be glad of the commission. She would call it Merlin's Cave, but she could not decide whether the style should be bizarre or conventional. She would have a frieze round the room of either Arthurian knights, or exotic dragons. Uther Pendragon, Arthur's father, had sported a dragon banner, and that fabulous animal could be very decorative. It would link up with Tintagel, where Arthur was supposed to have been born. Thus the morning passed, while she spun her daydreams, more profitable ones and more possible of achievement than dwelling upon what might have been.

Pluto hated David to be absent, and could rarely be coaxed to eat when the child was not there, so when Dick arrived all spruced up for the tea party, he suggested taking him with them. The dog was quite used to being left in a car, if the tea shop objected to his presence. When they had gone, Helen announced that she was going to put her feet up and have a good rest.

'What are you going to do?' she asked Damaris, 'go for a ride?'

'Yes, and I'll take the dogs.' She felt restless and unsettled, so she would go for a long excursion on to Bodmin Moor and tire herself out.

Helen's eyes fell on a brown paper parcel and she exclaimed:

'Oh dear, that's the jar we promised to send along to that artist type, he wants it for a composition he's working upon. Mary must have forgotten.' She smiled indulgently. 'She's very forgetful these days and then she pretends that she isn't in love.'

'I'll take it,' Damaris offered, 'it's only a step to Rose Cottage, and then I'll come back and change.'

'Oh, would you? That's kind of you, I'll have a cup of tea ready for you when you get back.'

Damaris stripped off her overall and picked up the parcel. She was wearing a skimpy crimplene frock, and the day being warm, she did not bother to put on a coat, nor did she bother to change her sandals; as she had said, it was only a step. Her dress was yellow, and with her russet hair blown by the wind, she looked not unlike an autumn leaf, as she flitted over the road with her parcel. She also looked absurdly young, without a trace of the stately young woman in white and silver who had gone to her birthday party.

Her way lay through a cluster of cottages, and along beside the river, with the steep slopes of Penally hill on the other side. They were very picturesque little cottages adorned with flowering plants, among which the ubiquitous red geranium gave a splash of colour against the whitewash. Among them was a rival souvenir shop, which Mary declared jealously had no 'class'. The little museum with its collection of mementoes of Cornish superstition stood end on to the lane. Damaris had visited it more than once and been intrigued by its symbols of ill-wishing. If she had lived a couple of hundred years ago, would she have made an image of Rosita and stuck it full of pins, and presented Mark with a love philtre? But philtres recalled his nonsense at Valmond and she thrust the thought away. Beyond the museum were more cottages including that occupied by the artist. He came in answer to Damaris' ring, a tall bearded youth in a paint-smeared smock, and was evidently in the throes of composition, so she did not linger. He grabbed the parcel, saying he had just reached the point when he needed the jar, and she bade him a hasty goodbye.

She had covered about half the distance back, when she came to an abrupt halt. A familiar figure was striding towards her and for a moment her heart stood still, while the usual sensation of near panic swept over her. So he had not given up the pursuit. Then her common sense reasserted itself; as Mary had said, she could not continue to play hide-and-seek, and she must control her silly nerves. She had no reason whatever to need to hide from Mark Treherne. As she had decided at Bude, he would only want to know when and how she would accept delivery of her possessions. So firmly repressing the instinct which urged her to fly back to Rose Cottage and seek sanctuary in the bearded one's studio, she squared her shoulders and went forward to meet Mark.

CHAPTER SEVEN

HELEN had told Mark where he would find Damaris, for since a meeting seemed inevitable, she decided that an encounter out of doors would be less embarrassing for the girl than a tête-à-tête inside. He had been intensely irritated by Damaris' elusiveness and Mr. Preston had given no real reason for her withdrawal, except one suggestion which he had not credited. None of the Treherne men had been remarkable for patience or forbearance and he was no exception, but he had determined to be gentle but firm with her when he finally located her. When he saw the figure coming towards him in her skimpy yellow frock and sandals, with windblown hair, she was so reminiscent of the child he had met upon the beach who had disconcerted him by her insistence that she was engaged to him that much of his annoyance evaporated. She was still very young, and he had perhaps frightened her. He planted himself squarely in her path and looked her up and down with the quizzical expression that she so disliked.

'Well, madam, so I've run you to earth at last.'

In spite of her resolution, Damaris quailed. There was something slightly menacing about the tall figure in front of her, and she knew that he had every right to feel annoyed. Summoning all her courage, she lifted her head defiantly.

'What a way to talk!' she told him. 'I'm not one of your foxes to be hunted down.'

His lip twisted. 'Exactly like a fox, red hair and all.'

'My hair's not red,' she protested, thinking that she had chosen an unfortunate simile; he was hunting her down. Forcing a smile, she went on sweetly, 'I'm sorry if

I've put you to any inconvenience. Mary did tell me you wanted to see me about something or other, but I didn't realise it was urgent.'

'You expect me to wait indefinitely for an explanation of your extraordinary conduct?' he asked her, his patience ebbing. 'What do you suppose my sister thinks? The de Costas? They're expecting to see you again.'

'I'm really not interested in their reactions,' she said with deliberate provocation, needled by the reference to the de Costas. Rosita would be delighted by the turn of events. 'As for an explanation, Mr. Preston must have communicated with you. Didn't he tell you everything?'

'He told me some rigmarole about wanting to back out, but he had previously told me that when he saw you in Geneva you were quite determined to go through with it.' She flushed miserably at the memory of that unhappy interview. 'What's the matter with you, Damaris?' he concluded. 'Got cold feet?'

His eyes seemed to pierce her like steel blades and he looked very big and formidable. Her confidence began to ooze away, but she faced him with feigned boldness.

'I asked him to terminate our engagement,' she said firmly, 'because I realise it was a mistake,' and saw his black brows knit over eyes that began to smoulder with rising anger.

'It takes two to make an engagement and two to break it,' he pointed out with grim emphasis. 'I'll not stand for any shilly-shallying, Damaris, so don't try to play hot and cold with me.'

'I'm not playing,' she retorted, 'I mean it, Mark. I've nothing more to say to you, so please go away.'

He gave an exclamation of exasperation, his limited patience exhausted. 'Don't be so silly,' he told her. 'You're behaving like a naughty child, and there's only one effective way of dealing with kids.'

She lifted her chin defiantly. 'I'm too old to spank.'

'Oh no, you're not, it's something I'd like to do right now.'

A group of children ran past them shouting. They stopped and turned to throw curious glances towards the angry man and the pale girl.

'We can't talk here,' Mark said impatiently. 'Come with me. I've got the car in the park.'

'Nothing would induce me to come with you,' she declared. She backed away from him and glanced round nervously for a refuge.

'You'll do as I say,' he said between his teeth. 'We've got to thrash this out. I'm not going to put up with the whims and fancies of a brat of a schoolgirl.'

As she turned to flee, he overtook her in two swift strides, and caught her arm in a firm grip.

'How dare you!' she gasped, her own temper rising, as she sought to free herself. Her eyes blazed, green fire meeting blue flame, as his hold tightened. 'Let me go, you're hurting me!' she cried fiercely.

'You deserve to be hurt. Will you come quietly or do I have to carry you?'

He looked quite capable of abducting her.

'That won't be necessary,' she said hastily, clutching at her dignity, 'I'll come.'

He propelled her vigorously back along the lane, across the main road and into the car park. The car was unlocked, and he opened the door with his free hand, bundling her into the passenger seat and shutting the door on her with a bang. She rubbed her bruised arm while he got in beside her, her temper boiling, her fury obliterating her fear. Mark slammed in the clutch and the car shot forward, nearly jerking her out of her seat. She glanced at the seat belt, but was too proud to put it on. If he wanted to risk killing her, she would not stop him. They tore up the hill out of the valley towards Stratton with increasing acceleration. This was Mark at his worst, domineering, trampling upon her susceptibilities, acting the bully.

He turned off the main road on to the narrow secondary one that followed the coastline, rising and dipping like a switchback. Luckily they did not meet another vehicle as the car hurtled on. Mark drove in silence, with compressed lips and a heavy scowl; it was she who broke the ominous quiet.

'At least you had the decency to come alone this time.'

'What do you mean?'

'You had Miss de Costa with you when you came before.'

'Why not? She knew where you lived, and I didn't. Did you expect me to search that rabbit warren of a place to locate you?'

She had not thought of that one. 'But Tom knew the house.'

'Tom had something else to do. Was I to disorganise all my staff because of your idiocy? Does it matter who came with me?'

'Oh, not at all.' If he could not see the enormity of his offence, she was not going to point it out. Silence fell again until the road reached a gate that barred progress, it continued over fields with a succession of gates that had to be opened and shut. They were in a deserted stretch of country that undulated away towards the moors on their right and the cliff tops on the left. Behind them was a glimpse of the sea, with the coast stretching to the promontory of Tintagel's rock. Directly below them was a whitewashed farm, around which red cattle were grazing. Mark stopped at the gate and cut his engine. Then he turned in his seat and looked at her, his eyes travelling from the tousled copper head to the small sandalled feet, and his lip curled sardonically.

'Well?' he said curtly.

'Well what?'

'What's made you change your mind?'

Very deliberately she told him, 'I happened to see

you kissing Rosita de Costa less than twenty-four hours after you'd got yourself engaged to me.'

'Is that all?' he said, and laughed. 'I'm afraid kissing pretty girls is rather a weakness of mine. It doesn't mean a thing, as you should know.'

He was right there, she did know that his kisses never meant anything. She stared rigidly ahead at the green field through the bars of the gate. Glancing at her stony profile, he added lightly:

'Nevertheless it was confoundedly careless of me to let you see the performance.'

'It wasn't so much what I saw as what I heard,' she returned. 'She...Rosita...said you loved each other and I was a funny child.'

'Well, aren't you?'

'Oh!' She clenched her hands. 'I—I hate you!'

'Maybe, but you're going to marry me. This thing's gone too far, Damaris, you'll make us the laughing stock of the county if you jilt me now.'

'I couldn't care less.'

'Then you've got to be made to care. What about Ravenscrag? I thought you were prepared to accept anybody in order to keep the place.'

'No, not anybody,' she said venomously. 'Not you.'

He turned from her abruptly. That one struck home, she thought triumphantly. They were now both so angry that their only desire was to hurt each other. His eyes fell upon her ringless hands clenched in her lap.

'What have you done with the ring and the diamonds? Pawned them?'

'Oh!' She flamed scarlet. 'How dare you say that! I ... I left them behind.' She had meant to tell him where, but she had forgotten all about them.

'Did you? Where?' Plainly he did not believe her. She told him.

'What a childish way to behave!'

'You're always harping on my childishness,' she cried fiercely. 'Obviously I'm not sophisticated enough for you. I'm too ignorant, and...' she recalled Rosita's words. 'I don't know what passion is.'

'That's soon remedied, my darling. I shall take great pleasure in teaching you.' He was smiling, but not pleasantly, and his eyes held the sardonic glint that she resented. As he reached for her, she struck him with all her strength across his mocking face. She saw the imprint of her hand clear on his brown cheek until the blood rose to obliterate it. She saw nothing else for some time. When at length he released her, she sat white and trembling in her seat, one hand to her bruised mouth, while Mark was breathing hard.

'I don't advise you to do that again,' he said thickly. 'I happen to have a hot temper.'

There was a long silence between them, broken only by the mournful cries of the gulls, while Mark mastered himself and she strove to control her trembling limbs. Then he said coldly:

'Sorry if I was rough, but you're enough to provoke the patience of an angel.'

'You're a brute,' she cried recklessly, 'a great, hulking bully!'

A gleam of appreciation showed in his eyes. She had a spirit as fiery and untamed as his own.

'Right,' he said coolly, 'granted I'm a brute and a bully and you hate me, but you'll stay engaged to me. Hang it all, girl, you've been telling me our marriage was what your grandfather, my great-uncle, wanted, ever since you met me, and you regarded his wish as sacred, or some such.'

Her lips quivered. 'He ... he thought you'd take care of me.'

'Well, haven't I done that? Sent you to the best school on the Continent, watched over you'—his lips twisted into an ironic grin. 'Even at Valmond.' She winced. 'You didn't think I'd let you go to stay with that little trollop Céleste without coming to see what you were up to?'

She flared up at that. 'How dare you call her names! If she made advances, you encouraged her.'

'We've been into that before. Didn't you put her up to it?'

That of course was correct.

'If you'd come in your true colours, it wouldn't have been necessary,' she pointed out. 'I thought you were a big, bad wolf and I was contracted to Cousin Mark.'

'Which you still are.' She was silent. She always had difficulty in reconciling the man beside her with her preconceived idea of Mark Treherne, that illusion had lasted too long to be easily dismissed.

A hawk was hovering overhead; as they both watched it, it swooped down upon some hidden prey.

'A merlin,' Mark said absently, 'he's got his dinner too,' as the bird rose with something in its claws. Damaris gave an involuntary shiver; Mark Treherne was not unlike a hawk.

'I'm sure Granddad had no idea you'd be ... like you are,' she told him.

'On the contrary, he knew very well what I'd be like. I'm a Treherne, and they've none of them been saints. They were even involved with the wreckers years ago, and they, you know, were a ruthless lot. I shouldn't be surprised if your beloved Ravenscrag hadn't been supported by their ill-gotten gains.'

Again Damaris shuddered. What Cornish man or woman did not know about the wreckers, those vultures who lured ships to their doom and were even guilty of throwing the wretched survivors back into the sea to ensure their silence. Often as a child, Mrs. Garth had entertained her with highly coloured accounts of their exploits.

'Jamaica Inn and all that,' she said. 'You fit into the picture exactly.'

'Thanks very much, but this is getting us nowhere. I can't understand you, Damaris. I thought when we were at Valmond,' he stopped and looked at her almost appealingly, 'didn't you have some softer feelings for me then?'

'For Christian Trevor,' she said, 'but he never existed, did he?'

He turned his face away and she thought she heard him swear under his breath.

'I don't like deceit,' she went on clearly, 'and whatever your motives, you did deceive me. You played with me—and dropped me.'

'I was going to pick you up again.'

'How was I to know that?'

'Did you really imagine I would let you go out of my life?' he asked.

'I did,' she said shortly. 'You see, I didn't know you were after Ravenscrag.'

'Charming opinion you've got of me!'

'You've done your best to earn it.'

He stared bleakly in front of him, biting his lips. She considered his profile, the straight nose, the forceful chin, the attractive way the crisp black hair grew above his ears. Child of a broken marriage, Elena had told her, who found difficulty in giving love and trust because love had been betrayed. He had never asked her for either, but could Rosita fulfil his need? The fact that she belonged to his mother's people and that their friendship was of long standing might give her a hold over him, but she had an intuition that he did not expect either from the Argentine. All he wanted was to slake his passion for her, and that was all he would ever ask from a woman.

Inconsequently, she said: 'Your parents weren't in love, were they?'

He looked at her in surprise, and his mouth set in a bitter line.

'Who's been talking?'

'Elena. Our marriage would have been like theirs, wouldn't it?'

'God forbid!' he ejaculated. 'It was because of the

162

misery my mother went through that I wanted to be sure...' he broke off. 'Oh well, never mind that now,' He clenched his fist on the steering wheel. 'Mr. Preston gave me a hint which I hadn't credited until now, but perhaps he's right. I suppose that on that trip to Paris you insisted upon...'

'How do you know about that?' she interrupted.

'Of course I knew, he told me.'

'You've no right to spy upon me!'

'Just now you said your grandfather expected me to look after you,' he reminded her. 'Do try to be consistent, my dear, but that's it, isn't it? You met someone there whom you've decided you prefer to myself.'

This assumption was so unexpected that she could only stare at him blankly. He took her silence for assent, and went on, 'This boy you were out with when I called—what was his name—something beginning with D. Who is he?'

Damaris drew a long breath. She saw in a flash that Mary's little joke had given her a chance to get her own back, to repay him for all the humiliation he had heaped upon her, to compensate for Rosita. If he could play a masquerade so could she.

'A very nice boy,' she said demurely. 'He loves me.'

'What does he do?' The question was sharp as a pistol shot. Remembering Dick Everett, she told him, 'He's a garage mechanic with good prospects.'

'Indeed? What was he doing in Paris?'

'People go to Paris for holidays,' she said vaguely.

'I see. Are you sure he isn't after your money?'

'He doesn't know I've got any. Most people in Boscastle think I'm Mary Brooke's assistant.'

His mouth turned down. 'What a set-up! Garage mechanics and shop assistants!'

'Genuine people,' she said firmly, 'and it doesn't matter what a man does when one's in love.'

'So you admit you love this young man?'

Thinking of David, she said simply, 'I adore him.'

His eyes searched her downcast face. 'Why didn't you tell me about this boy you—er—adore, before we went through all that mummery on your birthday?'

'How could I? I never saw you beforehand, and I didn't feel I was free; I mean—well, things seemed different then.'

'You mean before you discovered I was your Cousin Mark?'

'Partly,' she said unwillingly.

'But if I'd turned out to be the old gentleman you'd expected, you'd have gone through with it?'

'I don't know,' she cried wildly. 'It wasn't until I saw the Manor again that I realised everything was changed, it all seemed different...'

He smiled sadly. 'Everything changes, Damaris, it's always a mistake to go back.'

He was silent while she meditated upon the truth of his words. She had gone to Ravenscrag expecting to take up her life there where she had left off a year before, with Cousin Mark a substitute for her grandfather, but she had changed also. Ravenscrag no longer meant to her what it once had done, and she realised with a feeling of guilt that if Sir Hugh had still been alive, his sole companionship would no longer content her. Only Mark had not changed, he was still the same ruthless, imperious person whom she had met at Valmond, intent upon bending everyone to his will. That she was wrong about him his next words showed. He said quietly:

'You came looking for a reproduction of your grandfather and you found—me. Paradoxically I'm both too young for you and too old. Youth turns to youth, and twelve years can make a lot of difference. I had years of hard living while you were still in the nursery. Latin-Americans mature young.'

'I suppose that's it, you're too experienced for me,' she said drearily, but knew her statement was false. It was his maturity, his self-assurance that drew her youth. She took no interest in boys of her own age, who seemed to her to be raw, self-absorbed and callow. But Mark's amatory experiences were another matter, they were still going on.

Very gently he took her face between his hands. Startled, her eyes flew to his, but she could not sustain meeting his intent blue gaze that seemed to be trying to probe her very soul. Her lashes fell to veil her eyes.

'So—after the party you came to realise that even Ravenscrag couldn't compensate you for losing your love?' he asked her.

'I realised that the Manor couldn't compensate for—for everything,' she said truthfully.

He dropped his hands and sighed. 'No, property can't compensate for lack of love,' he admitted, and she wondered if Rosita had convinced him of the truth of that statement, but he would not have to give up Ravenscrag. She had renounced all claim to it, repudiating that clause in her grandfather's will.

'You should have told me as soon as you made your decision,' he rebuked her, 'instead of running away, and causing Mr. Preston and me so much misapprehension. But then you were always prone to running...' She heard the note of laughter in his voice and her heart quivered. Valmond and that magic night when she had run from him across a silvered lawn after he had kissed her, and the nightingale filled the air with melody, but when he had caught up with her, he had asked if she thought he would try to seduce Cousin Mark's fiancée. Recalling how he had played with her affections, while all the time his own were engaged elsewhere, she steeled herself against him.

'I thought if I went without telling you, it would save a lot of useless argument,' she said stiffly, 'and so it would have, if you hadn't been so...er...persistent.'

'I couldn't believe...' he broke off, and smiled wryly, 'but I wouldn't have argued. I know when I'm beaten.'

Again silence fell between them, while Mark seemed

to be thinking, his eyes fixed on the white clouds crossing the blue heavens. Damaris began to regret her
deception about David. She glanced furtively at Mark's
still face, which in repose looked a little sad. Her
temper had cooled to be replaced by a sense of loss. Her
heart was still drawn towards the man beside her, with
the unreason hearts are apt to show in spite of all the
prudence of the head. Acute misgiving assailed her.
Was she being an utter fool to throw away what she
most desired prompted by pique and pride? He was
still prepared to marry her, though he did not love her.
Should she not take him on his own terms while she
had the chance? She had only to confess that her
garage mechanic was a myth, agree to continue with
her engagement and hope for the best. He might tire of
Rosita in time, and the wife had the advantage of a
permanent tie. Helen had urged her to fight for what
she wanted, and she had told her that Mark was not
worth a battle. Deep in her innermost core, she knew
that that was not true. Mark had his faults, but he was
a strong man, a capable man, Ravenscrag would pros-
per under his control. Besides which he was a Treherne, they had a common heritage, and that should
help her to understand him and bind him to her.

Impulsively she touched his arm. 'Mark ...' then she
hesitated; capitulation was never easy. He turned his
gaze back to her, all temper and passion had died away
in him too. The blue eyes were kind, but remote.

'Excuse me, I was thinking,' he said with unusual
gentleness. 'If only you'd been frank with me, I would
never have forced my attentions upon you. You're
quite free to go to this boy, but with your permission
we'll allow the engagement to stand for a while, until
all the excitement has died down,' (Exactly what she
had suggested to Mr. Preston) 'then we'll quietly break
it off.'

She was too late, he had accepted her decision and
her lie. The opportunity of reconciliation had gone,

and now that his anger was spent, he was secretly relieved to be rid of her.

'And Ravenscrag?' she asked anxiously.

His face hardened. 'I shall sell it.'

'No!' she protested. 'No, Mark, you can't do that.'

'It's the only solution, Damaris. You couldn't live there, the house is too big for you to maintain, and you told me your man is a mechanic, not a farmer.'

'But you're a Treherne,' she faltered, 'the last one...'

'That doesn't mean much to me. In South America they call me Señor Tererno—the English consonants are too difficult for the Latin tongue. I shall be going back to Argentina for good.'

'And you'll marry Rosita?' she asked faintly.

'Possibly.'

So that was that. She ventured one last question.

'But if you'd married me, you'd have stayed in Cornwall?'

'Since I'm not going to marry you that contingency doesn't arise,' he said coldly.

She was silenced. A sensation of numbness crept over her, as he started the engine. She had obtained her freedom, she could now settle to her future with Mary and Helen as she had planned without any obstruction from him, but it seemed empty and dreary. He reversed the car and as they began the return journey, went on speaking in a voice devoid of expression.

'Half the proceeds from the sale will be yours, of course. Mr. Preston told me you wanted your horse, and she shall be sent to you at once. Anything else you'd like from the house can be delivered to you later on. I shall be seeing you from time to time and when I've found that confounded ring you've hidden away, you shall also have that. Please wear it on the appropriate finger until we've disposed of the fiction of this tomfool engagement. You can explain the necessity to that boy-friend of yours, if that isn't too much to ask of you.'

'No,' she whispered, feeling she could not bear to deceive him a moment longer, 'but, Mark, I...'

He went on as if she had not spoken. 'The diamonds I shall take back, if you'll forgive me. They aren't Treherne, they belonged to my mother.'

He wants them for Rosita, she thought despairingly. There was no point in confessing, he had worked everything out to his own satisfaction.

'Thank you, Mark,' she said meekly. 'Of course I don't mind about the necklace. You've been very generous.'

'Not at all. All I've offered to you is yours by right in justice if not at law.'

So he was salving his conscience by paying her off, as if money could compensate for heartache. She thought of the miles of ocean that would separate them, of Rosita waiting for his return at the other side of the world, and she had aided and abetted him by yielding to her own stupid stiff-necked pride.

He drove back to Boscastle at half the speed he had driven out. Thick hedges rose on either side of the narrow road, overhung with trails of honeysuckle now showing red berries. She saw them through a haze of tears; surreptitiously she wiped her eyes, hoping Mark would not notice, but there seemed no danger of that. He sat stony-faced beside her, his gaze fixed on the road ahead.

He drove into the car park and stopped.

'May I drop you here? It's the best place to turn.'

'Of course,' she said, opening the door.

Then he did look at her and his eyes were like blue ice.

'Goodbye, Damaris. You'll be hearing from me.'

'Goodbye, Mark.'

She walked slowly away as he went back up the road they had just traversed. During those last moments

168

while he had arranged her future he had been exactly as she had hoped Cousin Mark would be, kind, paternal and remote. Of the passion, the violence, the temper that she had seen from time to time, there had been no trace. He had released her without further argument, possibly with relief, and she was aware of an infinite regret.

As he had said, Damaris did continue to see Mark from time to time. He always made a point of ringing her up to make sure she was available before he appeared and their rendezvous was the car park. He firmly refused to enter or even to approach the shop. Mary, who noticed this, declared he was a snob, but that Damaris hotly denied. Whatever his reasons, Mark was no snob. He seemed to be trying to dissociate himself entirely from her personal life. She had to confess that she had nowhere to house Sheba, and it was he who arranged for the mare to be accommodated at a farm within easy walking distance of her home, and it was he who procured for her David's pony, when she mentioned that she wanted to buy one for a child in whom she was interested, insisting that she would be cheated if she tried to buy it herself.

'Being the little innocent you are, you'd be a horse-coper's natural prey,' he told her—a remark she took in good part.

He drove her to see Mr. Preston several times, since she had to sign documents to give him a clear title to the property before he could sell, and other papers, which Mr. Preston told her were to safeguard her own interests.

These visits too were strictly impersonal. Whatever his secret thoughts Mr. Preston was entirely business-like, but now and then when he thought he was unobserved, Damaris caught his gaze upon her with a slightly puzzled expression. Once when Mark emphatically reasserted that he would never return to England, he echoed Damaris' sigh.

The outings culminated in a coffee at a tea shop or a drink in a hotel lounge. That the preparations for the sale cost Damaris some natural pangs, both were aware, but neither ever referred to the matter beyond what was essential. She wondered often if he did not feel regret in parting with the place that had been his ancestors' home for generations, but he seemed to have no sentimental attachment to it whatever. His conversation was always about Argentina. He described to her the immense cattle farms, the miles of flat pampas, and the stark majesty of the Andes, which lay between it and Chile, mountains that made the Alps look like mushrooms, and the slopes of which were stark and unfriendly. He also described the gay life of Buenos Aires, and the not infrequent revolutions. She sensed he was deliberately detaching himself from his surroundings, and his spirit was already back in South America. Contact with him was bitter-sweet. Now that he was lost to her for ever, and no longer made frightening overtures, her old love for him revived. Without the galling presence of Rosita, it was easy to forget that he loved another woman. He had become the kind, considerate friend that she had hoped to find in Cousin Mark, but she also knew that such a relationship would no longer satisfy her. She wanted all or nothing, and nothing was what she was going to get. Often she longed to ask him about his future plans, even about his marriage, painful though that topic would be, but knew she could not do so. He avoided all intimate conversation, never asked what she was doing or hoped to do. The moment their talk veered towards the personal, he changed the subject. It was as though a wall of ice had risen between them, and though she had helped to erect it, perversely she longed to break it down. Once she said to him:

'After all, we're still cousins. Can't we be friends?'

'I thought I've been acting in a cousinly manner,' he

returned. 'I've given you all the help I can.'

'Yes, and I'm very grateful, but you're so distant, so...' She could not find the right word to express her meaning.

They were sitting in the lounge of a country inn on their way back from Launceston. Through the window, the distant tors of Dartmoor formed a sinister rampart against a sky banked with cloud. They looked forbidding, but no more so than Mark, as he said, 'My dear Damaris, don't be an idiot. Surely you realise it's impossible for us to be intimate now? You're the last person I could treat as a friend.'

She picked up her nearly empty wine glass, and became engrossed in its contents.

'I don't see why not.'

He looked at the inky crescents of her eyelashes, veiling her downcast eyes, the graceful curve of her neck under the molten copper curls. His hand clenched on the table edge.

'I should have thought it was obvious,' he said stiffly. 'Let's have another drink.'

He went towards the bar, and her eyes followed his lean, lithe figure, which his chunky sweater seemed to emphasise. He leaned carelessly on the counter talking to the barmaid with easy nonchalance. She was a pretty girl, and plainly captivated by Mark's charming smile. Damaris turned her gaze to the louring sky outside the window, thinking dismally that he had snubbed her because he could not forgive her for jilting him, even though he wanted to be free of her. His male vanity had been hurt because she had not found him irresistible.

Her great solace during those difficult days was the weekends, and Saturdays in particular, which day was devoted to horses and dogs. It was Mary's busiest day in the shop, the time when Helen did her baking, and David's holiday. He was completely fearless on the pony and was soon able to accompany Damaris when she wanted to go further afield. Together with their escort of dogs, they explored all the unmetalled lanes and open spaces in the neighbourhood where they could ride without traffic hazards. She was a little alarmed by the expense entailed in maintaining her 'stable', but with the promise of further funds due from the sale, she hoped to be able to afford it. The farmer who housed the horses was amused by the two young equestrians and was generous in the matter of fodder, and during the week, the weather being mild, the animals were out at grass.

'Yew don't need to give 'um much corn unless you be going to hunt,' he told her, 'makes 'um too skittish.'

Damaris assured him she had no intention of hunting and mild hacking at the weekends was all they could manage.

October came in and the leaves became tinged with amber and russet. Then one morning a car drew up at the door, and Elena de Costa got out of it.

Damaris had not seen her since her night at Ravenscrag. Mark never spoke of his visitors, and Damaris had appreciated his reticence. She had tried hard to forget that Rosita was still at the Manor and in daily contact with him. Elena looked very handsome in a black suit with a wide-brimmed Spanish-looking hat, encircled by a gilt cord, and a barbaric-looking gold ornament on her lapel. Damaris ran out to greet her, and was warmly embraced. Pedro waved to her from the car, but declined to come in, though Elena accepted Damaris' invitation with alacrity.

'We've come to say goodbye,' she told her. 'We go home the day after tomorrow.'

She seemed to fill Mary's tiny sitting room with her opulent presence. Damaris saw her glance towards her left hand which was adorned with the Treherne betrothal ring, but she tactfully did not refer to the broken engagement, though she must know the true state of affairs, neither did she mention Rosita. She looked about her with a slightly incredulous air and Damaris guessed she was wondering how any girl could endure such cramped quarters after the gracious spaciousness of the Manor. She speculated upon what exactly Mark had told her. Helen came in and was introduced and suggested that Elena might like to see the shop.

'Indeed I would,' Elena exclaimed. 'It must be so interesting.'

She certainly seemed to find it so, examining the local pottery and carving with delight. She bought several pieces to take home with her. Damaris wanted to make a present of them, but she insisted upon paying for them.

'It's your living,' she pointed out, 'you mustn't be too generous.'

Mary and Helen were charmed with her, and Elena seemed to be doing her best to please. She only once referred to what had occurred, and then obliquely.

'I'm sorry we haven't seen more of you,' she told Damaris, 'but Mark has been so busy, there's been so much to decide. It was difficult, you understand?'

'Indeed I do,' Damaris said with heightened colour. Elena gave her a long look and changed the subject.

When she came to take her leave, she said, 'I hope you'll come and stay with Pedro and me after Rosita is married. We'd love to have you.'

Damaris turned cold. So it was all settled. Mark had wasted no time. Not surprising that he had spurned her suggestion of friendship. He must have grudged the time he had to spend with her that took him away from the company of his beloved. She twisted the ring upon her finger; how irksome it must have been to him to see it there, since he could hardly give Rosita his pledge until he had severed himself from his previous tie.

She was aware of a dull ache in her heart, but she managed to smile brightly as she responded.

'It's very kind of you to ask me, but South America is a long way off.'

'Not really, jet flying has made the world shrink. We're your only relations, and having found you, little cousin, I don't want to lose sight of you.' She hesitated, wondering if Damaris would be offended if she offered to help with her fare, but decided that was something that could be settled later. Before she could issue a definite invitation, there would be all the performance of Rosita's wedding to be gone through with its invitations and ceremonies. Her sister-in-law insisted that it must be a memorable occasion and Argentine weddings were lush.

Damaris' eyes misted at Elena's words. 'It's sweet of you to say that, Elena,' she said huskily. 'I was afraid you'd be feeling sore with me—because of Mark.'

'What an idea!' Elena exclaimed briskly. 'That's nothing to do with me. I daresay the way things have turned out will be all for the best.'

A remark Damaris did not find very comforting.

'Is he staying on at Ravenscrag all alone?' she asked hesitantly.

'He'll have to until this tiresome business is fixed up. Lawyers are always so slow, aren't they? But he needn't wait for the actual sale. That mayn't be concluded for months. Those big old houses are rather white elephants nowadays.'

Damaris winced inwardly, wishing that she had not introduced the unhappy subject. She did not like to think of Mark left solitary at Ravenscrag, a stranger in a foreign country, but she was the last person who could offer him solace.

She went with Elena out to the car where Pedro was waiting, contentedly smoking a cheroot and reading a newspaper. He disposed of both when he saw her coming and sprang out to greet her.

'I regret we have done nothing to entertain you,' he said, bowing over her hand, 'but when you come to visit us it will be different. You will come, will you not? You will find Argentina an interesting country.'

She made a polite rejoinder, but it would be a very long time before she could bring herself to visit an *estancia* that lay side by side with the one where Mark and Rosita were, presumably, enjoying married bliss, even though the distance between the houses appeared to be considerable.

She watched them drive away, while she wondered if and when she would see them again.

Upon the next occasion when she had reason to meet Mark, she asked him if he were lonely now that his relations had gone home.

'It can be a bit melancholy up at the Manor at this time of the year,' she told him.

'Is it?' he returned with his characteristic sardonic smile. 'I haven't noticed it. I'm enjoying a little peace and quiet, and there's always plenty of hunting and shooting.'

A look of distaste crossed her face. 'Blood sports! I hate creatures being killed.'

'You're too squeamish. Everything has to die, sooner or later.'

As time went by, she saw less and less of him, as was only to be expected. Mary asked her if it was not time that the myth of the engagement was finally dispelled. Several acquaintances were putting out feelers regarding wedding presents, and she did not know how to put them off.

'It'll be soon now,' Damaris told her with a constriction round her heart, for when the final break came, her last link with Mark would be severed.

Inevitably the day came when he told her curtly that the legal business had been completed and arrangements made to advertise the sale.

'You must come up to the Manor and pick out any pieces you may like to keep,' he told her. 'I'll arrange a convenient day with Mrs. Garth and she'll give us lunch.'

He had met her as usual at the car park, and she was sitting in the front seat of the stationary car, while he lounged against the bonnet beyond the open door, smoking one of his favourite Turkish cigarettes, the scent of which always recalled nostalgic memories of Christian and Valmond. Dully she thanked him, adding wistfully, 'I'll be glad of a chance to say goodbye to the old place.'

'Oh, come, it isn't going to be pulled down,' he said with a laugh. 'It might even be taken over by the National Trust. Then you can visit it whenever you wish for a payment of four bob a time. Perhaps I should leave the family portraits for the public to gape at. Too bad to cart them over to South America to be eaten by ants.'

'How can you joke about it?' she asked in a choked voice.

He threw down his cigarette butt and stamped upon it as carelessly as he was trampling upon her feeling for Ravenscrag.

'Snap out of it, girl,' he admonished her, 'don't sound so tragic. This isn't a tragedy, in fact it has all the elements of farce.' He opened his case and abstracted another cigarette. 'Aren't you glad this impossible situation is nearly ended? I know I am. It must have been an even greater strain for you than it's been for me. Once the sale notices are up, pussy will be out, and you can dispose of that bit of junk on your finger.'

Involuntarily she glanced at the sapphire upon her left hand. He had bent his head to light his cigarette, his face turned away from her, and he appeared to be infinitely remote. She wished he would enter the car and sit beside her, but he always avoided intimacy as much as possible and never touched her if he could help it. Once he had ushered her inside, he had assumed his unfriendly stance between windscreen and bonnet. He seemed to be in a curious mood, restless, derisive, with an undercurrent of something which she would have diagnosed as bitterness, if she had not known he was soon to be reunited with Rosita and had more cause for rejoicing than bitterness.

'Yes, it'll be a relief to do that,' she said with a false brightness to conceal the desolation in her heart. 'I hate any sort of deception.'

He threw a brief glance in the direction of her downbent head, then looked away.

'Okay, you needn't rub it in,' he said, and she flushed, realising that he thought she was referring to his own performance at Valmond which she had long ago forgiven.

'Sorry I'll have to leave you to face the music alone,' he went on, 'but the gossip will soon die down. I must say your young man has been most complaisant. I wouldn't have allowed my girl to wear another man's ring for any reason whatever.'

She started. She had forgotten her little fiction about David. Of course that was the reason why he would never come near the house. He did not want to encounter her supposed suitor.

'That's all I wanted to tell you,' he concluded. 'I'll phone you when I've fixed a date with Mrs. Garth. I suppose you can come any time?'

'Yes,' she whispered.

'Good. After that you won't have to see me again.'

The words sounded in her ears like the knell of doom. Across the stream the breeze whispered in the trees, and the leaves drifted down. How melancholy the autumn season could be, the end of summer's blooming, the death of springtime's hopes.

He looked at her questioningly, holding the door, waiting for her to alight. Despondently she crept out of the car that had witnessed so many crises in her life. As she did so, she brushed against him, and he hastily drew back. Was her touch so obnoxious to him?

'Au revoir,' he said casually. 'Next time it'll be good-bye.'

She would not part from him allowing him to believe her foolish lie, one that was greater than the ring upon her finger.

'Please, Mark,' she said desperately, 'before you go I want to tell you about this boy, this Da...'

Abruptly he cut her short. 'Please, I don't want to know anything about him. When I'm gone you can put me and everything to do with me behind you and make a fresh start. It's what I intend to do.'

With Rosita, she thought. Her impulse to enlighten him died away. It would make no difference if she did tell him, he would treat it as another joke, another example of her childishness. Better let him continue to believe that she had a devoted admirer, and not suspect that she was hankering after him. Sadly she walked away without looking back.

It seemed that Damaris' new possessions were likely to be an embarrassment, as there were several pieces of furniture that she wanted to rescue from the sale at the Manor. Mary, however, had resolved her doubts, and she and Dick were only waiting for a house before getting married. The removal of her effects would make room for Damaris' things, and meanwhile she could store them. But although their living accommodation was thus confined, the shop possessed a fairly ample yard at the back, and a large outhouse, containing an old copper, dating from the period when extensive laundry was done at home. This provided a kennel for the dogs and looked like being their permanent home since Ravenscrag was denied them. Pluto had grown into a large leggy whelp, and Mary sometimes regretted Damaris' generosity, particularly when David had had him in the house, and she discovered that he had chewed up her slippers or destroyed a pair of tights. David loved the beast even more than his pony, there being between dog and boy a close affinity. He looked forward to Saturdays when, with both dogs and horses, Damaris took him for a long ramble.

It was therefore unfortunate that Mark chose a Saturday for Damaris' visit to Ravenscrag, and in her agitation at the prospect of this final ordeal, she forgot that David would be defrauded of his usual morning outing, until Mark had rung off. With a heavy heart she realised that it would be the last time that she would see him.

Placating David was difficult, he considered that she had let him down, although she assured him that it would only occur that once. Then he clamoured to be taken with her to Ravenscrag, and she had to tell him firmly that was impossible. Mark would object, or if he did not, he might realise that David was the boy whose name began with D. whom she had told him she adored. She felt she would need the support of that fictitious suitor to bolster her ego when they arrived at the Manor with its unpleasant reminder of the Rosita–Mark combination that had so wounded her. The time for telling him the truth was long past.

To a child the present is everything, and David was not entirely pacified by her promise of a ride on Sunday, and no more Saturday engagements.

'There's no school, and Mummy and Auntie Helen are always busy on Sat'days,' he complained, 'and Dick's no good, it's his busy day too.'

'I'll be back during the afternoon,' she pointed out. 'Perhaps we'll have time to take the dogs for a run.'

With which suggestion he had to be content.

But by the following afternoon she would have looked her last upon Mark Treherne, a whole phase of her existence would have ended, and she faced a blank future in which neither he nor Ravenscrag would have any part.

Nevertheless, she was determined to put on a brave show. She would hate Mark to realise what an ordeal he was putting her through. She could well imagine his quizzical expression at any sign of emotion she might betray. If he expected to achieve a subtle revenge for her treatment of him, she would disappoint him. She would be cool, aloof and strictly practical, and she prayed that Mrs. Garth would have the tact not to regale her with lamentations. But she could not indulge in them in Mark's presence, and she would endeavour not to be left alone with her. To sustain her poise, she must look her best. She carefully pressed her best suit, of fine green woollen mixture, and selected a white silk blouse to wear with it. She decided upon brown suede shoes, gloves and bag, and a smart little brown hat with a green felt flower that exactly matched her suit. There must be no trace of the *gamine* he had first known, above all she must be elegant in looks and manner. She looked doubtfully at her ring—the piece of junk, he had called it. She found she was very reluctant to take it off, but she could still wear it, he had told her it was hers, though not of course on the significant finger. For the present it could stay where it was. Until after tomorrow, she was still officially engaged.

Before going to bed, she washed and set her hair, a tedious chore, for there was a great deal of it. Perhaps she would have it cropped, she thought, it would be much less bother, and there would be no need to look feminine when Mark had gone. Finally she went to bed early to be well rested for the morrow that would tax all her endurance. She had no premonition that the dreaded expedition would not take place.

CHAPTER EIGHT

When that controversial Saturday morning dawned, the whole countryside was enveloped in a thick blanket of sea fog, which obscured the hills and filled the valleys with soft, grey vapour. Damaris began to wonder if Mark would be able to make it. Even he could not command the vagaries of the British climate. Throughout breakfast David gave her reproachful glances, and when she pointed out that the weather was not fit for riding, he insisted that the mist would soon clear and the day be bright, which was more than a little doubtful. Mary told him sharply not to worry poor Ris, who she could see was on edge, and he subsided sulkily. Then came the devastating discovery that Pluto was missing. Always an adventurous animal, he had found an opportunity to slip through the house and out on to the road. When he did not return for all their calling and whistling, Damaris greatly feared that he had been run over, though naturally she did not say so to David. She did her best to console him, saying the whelp was sure to turn up eventually, but it was no use going to look for him, as they had no idea in which direction he had run.

'If he doesn't come home soon, we'll ring up the police and they'll find him,' she promised, wondering what would be discovered and how she would cope with David's distress if the worst had happened.

As it turned out it was not on Pluto's account that the police were notified.

An unexpected spate of customers arrived at the shop, some belated coach party, which, finding the countryside obscured, were glad to spend the morning exploring the amenities of Boscastle and buying souvenirs. Damaris, while helping Mary to deal with them, thought David was with Helen. Helen, engaged with domestic chores, believed the child was with her. It was not until nearly midday, when Damaris was going up stairs to change for her meeting with Mark, that they discovered David was missing.

'He'll have gone to look for his dog,' Damaris exclaimed, while a distraught Mary in her turn suggested phoning the police.

'We'd better have a look round first,' said Helen. 'He might be with Dick.'

But Dick had not seen him.

They were in the midst of a worried consultation when Mark for the first time walked into the shop, it being long past the hour when Damaris should have met him at the car park. She stared at him blankly, while Mary and Helen retreated. He looked very tall and very out of place amid Mary's fragile merchandise.

'I . . . I didn't think you'd come,' she stammered, 'the fog . . .'

'Of course I've come, what's a bit of mist? I told you Mrs. Garth would be expecting you for lunch, and we'll be very late. You don't seem to be ready.'

He was staring in surprise at her very unready appearance. She had just returned from the Everetts'. She wore an old plastic mac over jeans and a jersey and her ruffled hair was wet with mist, her face pale with anxiety.

She passed her hand over her face. 'I'd forgotten all about it.'

'So it seems. Well, hurry up, I can't hang about all day.' He sounded brusque.

'I can't possibly come with you now,' she told him, 'something's happened.'

His manner changed and he looked concerned. 'I was afraid it might. What's the trouble?'

'David's lost.'

'David?' He frowned at the name.

'Yes, Mary's little boy. He's been gone for hours.'

His face cleared. 'David's a child?'

'Of course.' She had no thought for any subterfuge now. 'Oh, Mark, he's only five, and in this mist he may fall down a cliff or get run over . . .' her voice broke on a sob.

Instantly he was by her side, a sustaining arm about her, and she clung to him glad of his support and the comfort of his presence.

'Don't upset yourself, we'll find him,' he said gently. 'Now, when was he missed, and what have you done?'

From then on he took command, telephoning the police, who promised to organise a search with beaters and tracker dogs. He also rang all the local hospitals. Then he suggested that Helen made coffee for them all and they had some food.

'You must keep your strength up,' he told them kindly. Helen saw the wisdom of his suggestion, but Mary was too upset.

'We can't sit about doing nothing,' she objected, 'and food would choke me.'

'Much better leave the search to the professionals,' he told her. 'It won't help if you go and fall over a cliff, but you could get a bed ready with plenty of hot water bottles. He'll be chilled when they do find him,' then as Mary turned to the stairs, 'but do try to drink something first.'

It was he who took the cup of coffee Helen had brewed and coaxed her into swallowing it, while Damaris watched amazed by this new facet of Cousin Mark. All three women had automatically turned to him for guidance and were thankful he was there.

Tris and Sol, sensing something was wrong, were howling dolefully, and Damaris let them into the house. Surprisingly they seemed to recognise Mark, and fawned upon him delightedly. A thought struck him.

'Are they any good at tracking?'

'I don't know, but they might be,' Damaris said doubtfully, 'they just might.'

But they were not. Damaris put them on a coupling lead, showed them some of David's clothing, and said encouragingly, 'Find David,' but after casting around the front garden and the road beyond, while their hopes were raised, the dogs sat down and looked at her reproachfully. What sort of a walkie was this?

Discouraged, Damaris and Mark went indoors, when a whining and scratching at the door announced that Pluto had come back. He came in wet with mist and mud and crawled obsequiously on his belly, well knowing that he had sinned and craving for forgiveness. Where he had been or what he had been up to they had no means of knowing. They accepted his contrition, they had no heart to punish him. Damaris dried him and put down a bowl of food for him, but he would not touch it. Instead he whined and started padding round the room.

'He's looking for David,' Mary told them with a catch in her voice. 'He's always restless when he's out.'

'Then let him look outside,' Mark suggested.

Damaris put on his lead and watched anxiously as he cast around as his parents had done. Then he set off, tugging at the lead so that Damaris had to run to keep up with him, aware that Mark was striding along beside her. The animal crossed the road and led them towards the harbour, while Damaris' heart sank, but to her relief Pluto, nose to ground, turned up between two cottages away from the water and began to climb. Now the houses were below them, and the mist enclosed them, they could not see where they were or where they were going; all they knew was that they were moving steadily upwards. Wet fronds of dead bracken soaked through Damaris' trousers, rock outcrops bruised her fingers as she caught at them with her free hand to steady herself, thankful that Mark was behind her to catch her if she fell. The curtain of grey mist cut off visibility to less than a yard ahead.

She heard Mark say, 'I hope he knows what he's doing and this isn't a wild goose chase.'

'He does,' she answered, her eyes on the flagging tail, the muzzle close to the earth.

'I hardly think a child could climb up here,' Mark objected, and swore as a shower of shale descended upon him, dislodged by her impetuous progress.

'Sorry, Mark, I couldn't help it,' she gasped. 'I can't see a thing.'

'Don't waste breath upon apologies, you'll need it.' He sounded curt with anxiety.

The dog suddenly pulled so hard that the lead was jerked out of her hand, and she fell flat on her face, slithering backwards. Mark caught her, picking her up and setting her on her feet. The dog had vanished. She clung to him crying hysterically:

'Suppose he fell!'

'He didn't,' Mark reassured her, for through the mist they heard a shrill childish voice from above them crying joyfully, 'Pluto! Oh, Pluto!'

With his arm around her, Mark guided Damaris towards the sound. Under an outcrop of rock was a narrow ledge upon which David was crouched with his arms round Pluto's neck, being copiously licked by his rescuer. Damaris slid from Mark's hold and collapsed beside him.

'Oh, Davy, Davy, why did you scare us so?'

'I wanted to find Pluto,' the boy said. 'He often runs up here when we take him out, but he wasn't here and I was afraid to come down, 'cos I couldn't see nothing . . .' he dissolved into tears. 'I was so . . . frightened.'

'You're all right now,' Damaris told him, drawing him into her arms. She looked up at Mark, a dark pillar swathed in mist. 'But how on earth are we going to get down?' The ascent had been bad enough, the descent would be worse.

Mark sat down beside her, the ledge was just wide

enough for the three of them if they sat very close, and the dog.

'I think we'd better stay here until the searchers find us,' he suggested, 'we don't want to fall over a rock face, and Pluto evidently doesn't intend to guide us.'

The whelp, tired with his exertions, content to have found his master, had curled up on the skirt of Damaris' mac and gone to sleep.

'Not very comfortable, though,' he went on, 'and you're wet and cold. Have my coat.'

'No, you need it yourself, and my jersey's thick,' but she was shivering.

With difficulty in the confined space Mark removed his coat; it was a thick raincoat, and he draped it round their joint shoulders.

'We can share it,' he told her. The four of them huddled together under its shelter. Damaris had David on her knees, the dog was beside her, a patch of steaming warmth against her legs, and Mark put his arm around her waist.

'I'se hungry,' David whimpered.

'I'm afraid we can't do anything about that,' Mark said gently, 'but help will come soon. Try to go to sleep.'

He dozed off, while Damaris tried to ease her cramped position; Mark's arm tightened, drawing her against his shoulder.

'Lean on me,' he said.

She relaxed against him. His closeness, the assurance of his protective strength was very comforting.

'I gather that small person is the David you adore,' he said drily. 'Why did you try to mislead me?'

'I wanted to pay you out for Rosita,' she said frankly. 'I know it was silly, and I've been sorry ever since.'

'So you jolly well ought to be. As for Rosita, I don't suppose it's ever occurred to you that a man's in rather a difficult position when a woman throws herself at his head, especially when she's a guest in his house and a connection by marriage.'

'But ... but when I asked you, you said you were going to marry her.'

'I said no such thing. The actual word I used was "possibly", which means anything or nothing. You hadn't been very nice to me, had you, darling?'

'Oh, Mark,' she whispered, 'what a fool I was...' then she remembered something else. 'But Elena said she was going to be married, she asked me to stay with them after her wedding, and of course I thought she was marrying you. Was there ... is there someone else?'

'Definitely. Rosita has many strings to her bow,' he said drily. 'When I had told her very firmly it was no use wasting her time on me, she saved her face by informing me she was going to marry a certain Manuel Ramos, a match Pedro has been trying to arrange for some time.'

'But ... but didn't you have an affair with her? Elena said...'

He shifted under her weight, drawing her closer.

'Must you keep quoting my sister? She's not infallible. I wouldn't be such a fool as to have an affair on my own doorstep.' A remark which by its very cynicism carried conviction. 'Damaris, am I right in thinking that you're jealous?'

'So what?' she asked defensively.

'No one is jealous if they're indifferent.'

'I've never been indifferent to you,' she said, so low that he had to bend his head to catch her words. 'I've been furious with you, hated you, I've even ... loved you...'

'Loved me?'

'An idiotic schoolgirl's crush ... which I've tried to squash.'

'But why?'

'Because ... because you've never, ever, suggested you loved me.' Her voice died away as she buried her face in his shoulder.

187

He was silent for some moments, then he spoke with uncharacteristic diffidence. 'I don't know about this love business, Damaris, love can mean so many different things, but what I feel for you is something I've never felt for any other woman—of course I'm bound to say that,' he laughed, 'but it's true nonetheless. There have been other women, but never serious. We parted without regrets, but when you wanted to break our engagement, my life seemed utterly empty. I only let you go because I believed your happiness lay elsewhere.'

The child stirred and whimpered. Pluto uncurled and pricked up his ears, while Damaris raised her head.

'He's heard something,' she said. 'Hadn't you better shout? Your voice'll carry better than mine.'

'Before I do,' he said coolly, 'will you come back to me, Damaris? At Valmond I thought that at least you liked me. I planned a glad reunion when I unmasked, but everything went wrong. I believe you couldn't forgive me for not being old and decrepit as you expected.'

There was a hint of laughter in his voice. Damaris, her ears straining to hear the approach of the rescue party, tried to explain.

'I thought I could cope with an elderly man, and you had made me look rather a fool. Then there was Rosita . . .'

'Damn Rosita! Well?'

'You're selling Ravenscrag.'

'I don't want to sell it, but I couldn't bear to live there without you.'

There was a sound of movement below them, men's boots scraping on rock. She lifted her head to call to them, but Mark put his free hand over her mouth.

'Answer me first,' he commanded.

Through his fingers, she whispered, 'Blackmail?'

'Yes, confound it, blackmail.'

She pulled away his hand. 'Then I've no option,

188

have I, Mark? I . . . I'll be only too happy to come back to you.'

Pluto began to bark.

Later, much later, when they had disposed of the much needed meal that Helen had had ready for them, Damaris said:

'I'll take back what I said at Valmond. You're not so unlike Tristram after all.'

'Whatever made you think of that?'

'Echoes from the Château. But I didn't need a love philtre, Mark, only, like Iseult, I dared not name my— love.'

'About the first nice thing you've said to me,' he commented, and then Mary came in, having put David to bed.

'He wants to see you both before he'll settle,' she told them. 'Do you mind?'

They stood hand in hand beside Mary's bed in which David had been placed instead of the little camp one behind a screen in the corner where he normally slept. He was enjoying the importance of being a spoilt invalid, sitting propped up by the pillows, the remains of his supper on a tray beside him, while Pluto, from whom he had refused to be parted, lay stretched on the mat beside the bed, feebly flagging a tail, too weary to stand up to greet the visitors. David stared up at Mark, hero-worship shining in his eyes.

'When I'm a big man, shall I be like you?' he asked.

'I hope you'll be a better man than I am,' Mark said gravely.

That was beyond him. 'I likes you,' he announced.

'That's fine, son,' Mark told him, 'because you're going to see a lot of me when I marry Damaris.'

'And you'll take me to that Raven place, where Ris said I couldn't come?' the child asked anxiously.

Mark pressed Damaris' hand. 'You can spend all the time you like at Ravenscrag,' he said. 'You can be big brother to our kids when they come along.'

The eyes he turned to Damaris were blue flame, and she blushed scarlet. David sank back on his pillows, his lids dropping over his sleep eyes.

'Goody,' he murmured, then raised himself again to ask, 'but what do I call you? Are you a sir ... or an uncle?'

'Neither,' Mark declared firmly. 'Definitely I'm not a sir, and I don't feel avuncular, makes me seem old,' he shot a barbed glance at Damaris. 'I've been rejuvenated. How about Cousin Mark?'

By popular demand...

24 original novels from this series—by 7 of the world's greatest romance authors.

These back issues have been out of print for some time. So don't miss out; order your copies now!

Harlequin Reader Service
ORDER FORM